The Pieces We Mend

Laurel Ridge Series, Book #12

Tara Baisden

Sterling Ridge Press LLC

Copyright

Cover designed by Sterling Ridge Press LLC

Published by: Sterling Ridge Press, LLC www.sterlingridgepress.com

ISBN: 978-1-966093-28-2 Printed in the United States of America

First Edition: July 2025

For permissions, contact: tara@tarabaisden.com or visit www.tarabaisden.com

Also by Tara Baisden

<u>Riverbend Valley Series</u>

#1 A Cowboy's Second Chance

#2 Wanderlust & Wild Horses

#3 Heartstrings on the Horizon

#4 Runaway in Riverbend Valley

#5 Mended Hearts

#6 Healing Hearts

<u>Laurel Ridge Series</u>

#1. Season of Hope

#2. Finding Grace

#3. His Perfect Plan

#4. Love Redeemed

#5 Snowbound Blessings

#6 Sheltered Hearts

#7 Restoring Faith

#8 Love Rekindled

#9 Where She Belongs

About The Author

Tara Baisden is a Contemporary Christian Inspirational Romance author who proudly calls the beautiful state of West Virginia her home. Nestled on a sprawling mountainous property, she is surrounded by the peace and serenity of nature. Her days are happily spent in the quiet of country life, writing heartwarming stories of love, faith, and second chances. Tara also enjoys quilting, working in her garden, tending to her beloved pets, and soaking in the beauty of her surroundings.

With deep roots in West Virginia, family is everything to Tara. One of her favorite pastimes is gathering on the front porch with loved ones, sharing stories, laughter, and enjoying the simple, meaningful moments that life offers. When she's not crafting her novels, Tara can often be found exploring the rich history of her home state, visiting local historical sites, and, of course, stopping by every bookstore she passes! Her passion for reading and discovery always fuels her next adventure.

Tara is the author of the Laurel Ridges series of novels, as well as the Riverbend Valley series of novels, of which have been beloved by fans of inspirational romance. Her novels reflect her love for faith, family, and the timeless beauty of the world we live in.

Known for her sweet and clean romances, she creates characters that feel like family and settings that make readers want to visit again and again.

You can find out more about Tara and her latest releases at www.tarabaisden.com or follow her on social media for updates and behind-the-scenes glimpses of her writing process. Stay connected—you won't want to miss the heartfelt stories of love and family she has in store!

About Laurel Ridge

Welcome to the fictional town of Laurel Ridge, West Virginia!

Nestled deep in the heart of the Appalachian Mountains, Laurel Ridge is a place where time slows down, allowing visitors and residents alike to enjoy life's simple pleasures. With its quaint, brick-paved streets, historic storefronts, and the ever-present backdrop of rolling hills and dense forests, Laurel Ridge is a hidden gem that attracts tourists looking for both serenity and adventure.

<u>A Rich History</u>

The town was founded in the early 1800s by pioneering settlers who were drawn to the fertile land and abundant natural resources of the region. Laurel Ridge began as a small logging community, relying on the towering forests that covered the surrounding mountains. The New River, one of the oldest rivers in the world, provided an essential transportation route for lumber, as well as a lifeline for the early settlers.

As the years passed, the town evolved from a logging outpost into a thriving hub for craftspeople and artisans. By the late 19th century, it had developed a reputation for its hand-crafted furniture, textiles, and pottery, all made by skilled locals. The town's proximity to the New River also made it a destination for adventurous souls seeking to kayak, fish, or hike along the riverbanks.

A Place of Renewal

Though the logging industry faded by the early 20th century, Laurel Ridge adapted to the changing times. Its natural beauty and deep connection to West Virginia's mountain heritage drew travelers from near and far, transforming it into a beloved tourist destination. Local shops, run by generations of the same families, line the town square, offering handmade goods, locally sourced foods, and, most of all, warm hospitality.

The town's signature event, the Harvest Festival, began in the 1930s, celebrating the craftsmanship, music, and traditions passed down through the generations. Each year, visitors flock to enjoy live Appalachian music, taste locally grown produce, and witness demonstrations of old-world techniques like blacksmithing and weaving.

A Town of Faith and Community

At the heart of the town stands Laurel Ridge Community Church, a small, white clapboard building with a steeple that reaches toward the sky. Built in 1876, the church has been a pillar of faith and strength for the community for over a century. Its bell, crafted by the town's original blacksmith, has been ringing on Sunday mornings ever since, calling townsfolk to worship and reminding everyone of the enduring values of faith, hope, and love.

The church's history is intertwined with the town's, serving as a refuge in difficult times and a gathering place in moments of joy. Over the years, the church has grown to include an outreach center that supports local families and tourists in need, providing everything from free meals to spiritual counseling. The church's welcoming atmosphere reflects the town's deep sense of unity and service.

A Growing Tourist Haven

Today, Laurel Ridge has grown to a population of around five thousand people, yet it has managed to retain its small-town charm.

Dedication

For the brave hearts who have mended their own fences and learned to
stand tall in the storms.
This story is for you.
May you find a love as steady as the mountains, a friend who always
shows up with flowers and hard truths, and the sweet, surprising grace
of a butterfly landing on your heart just when you need it most.
And may you never forget that your story isn't over—God is just
getting to the good part.
Love, Tara

Contents

Chapter 1

Sheriff Mitch Baker pushed open the door to Martha's Diner, the bell above the door jingling, announcing his arrival. The morning crowd—mostly regulars with a smattering of summer tourists—looked up briefly before returning to their conversations.

"Well, if it isn't Laurel Ridge's finest." Martha Kincaid's voice carried over the clatter of dishes and morning chatter. She stood behind the counter, coffeepot in hand, her silver hair caught up in its usual practical twist. "You're looking a mite tired this morning, Sheriff. Late night?"

Mitch slid onto his usual stool at the counter. "Paperwork. Tourist season means more incident reports."

"Cream?" she asked as she poured him a cup of coffee.

"Black's fine."

"Usual breakfast?" She already had her order pad out, pencil poised.

"Please." He took another sip, letting the rich bitterness coat his tongue. "How's business going?"

"Busy enough to keep these old legs complaining, not so busy that I'm ready to retire to Florida."

"You'd be bored within a week if you retired."

"Three days, tops." Martha laughed. "Besides, if I retired, who'd feed you? Lord knows, you'd forget to eat if someone didn't put a plate in front of you."

Mitch smiled. "I manage."

"Cereal isn't managing, Mitchell Baker. It's surviving." Martha shook her head as she called his order back to the kitchen. "My Scottie always said a man who doesn't eat a proper breakfast starts his day off on the wrong foot."

The mention of her late husband softened her voice. Fifteen years a widow, and she still spoke of him like he might walk through the door any minute.

"Scottie was a wise man." Mitch glanced around the diner, taking in the familiar faces. Dorothy Henderson and her morning Bible study group occupied the corner booth, Bibles open beside coffee cups. The Williams sat at their usual table by the window, Mr. Williams reading sections of the newspaper aloud to his wife of fifty-seven years. A family of tourists studied a trail map of the New River Gorge, their excitement of adventure evident in their animated gestures.

Martha returned with a steaming plate of eggs, bacon, and home fries. "So, what's the verdict on the new deputy? Is she settling in okay?"

"She's good. Quick learner, good instincts." He cut into his eggs, the yolk running golden across the plate. "Deputy Dunbar's showing her the ropes."

"Reed's a good boy. Gets that steady nature from his daddy." Martha refilled his coffee without being asked. "Speaking of the Reed Dunbar, did you see his daddy's new book is out? Cozy mystery set right here in Laurel Ridge—though he calls it 'Pine Valley' in the books."

"Haven't had much time for reading lately."

"All work and no play, Sheriff." Martha tsked, wiping down the counter. "The Lord rested on the seventh day, you know. Even gave us a commandment about it."

"I'll take it under advisement."

The bell over the door jingled again, and Earl Smith's stocky frame appeared. The hardware store owner spotted Mitch and nodded, making his way to the counter.

"Morning, Sheriff. Martha." Earl settled onto the stool next to Mitch. "Coffee please."

"Good mornin' to you as well," Martha said as she poured his coffee.

Earl took a sip and sighed with appreciation. "The tourist season's booming this year. Sold out of fishing tackle twice this week already."

"Tourists are good for business," Mitch commented.

"Good for the town," Earl agreed. "Though my back disagrees when I'm unloading those supply trucks." He rotated his shoulder with a grimace. "Getting too old for this."

"You've been saying that since I was in high school," Mitch reminded him.

"And I've been right every year since." Earl grinned, the lines around his eyes deepening. "How's that brother of yours doing? Saw him out jogging the ridge trail yesterday. The boy moves like he's still in the military."

A familiar concern settled in Mitch's chest. "Cody's adjusting. Civilian life takes time."

Earl nodded, understanding in his eyes. "Well, tell him to stop by the store. I could use some extra muscle. It might be good for him to keep busy... something to focus on."

"I'll pass that along. Thanks, Earl."

"It's the least I can do. Your daddy helped me start my store when nobody else would give me a loan." Earl's voice held the quiet reverence that always accompanied mentions of Mitch's father. "Your daddy was a good man."

"That he was." Mitch said as he pushed his empty plate away.

Martha swooped in to clear his plate. "More coffee?"

"Better not. I should get back to work."

She nodded, sliding his check across the counter. "Take a couple of these for the road." She placed two muffins in a paper bag. "Blueberry. Fresh this morning."

"Martha—"

"Don't 'Martha' me. Someone's got to make sure you eat." She pushed the bag toward him.

Mitch accepted the bag with a nod of thanks, knowing better than to argue.

"You stay safe out there," Martha said.

"Always do." He stood, adjusting his duty belt. "Earl."

"Sheriff." Earl raised his coffee mug in salute.

Outside, the July heat hit him like a brick wall, the humidity typical for a West Virginia summer. Main Street bustled with morning activity, shopkeepers sweeping sidewalks, early shoppers wandering between stores, and locals going about their routines.

Mitch walked across Main Street to his patrol truck, the white Laurel Ridge Sheriff's Department logo gleaming in the sunlight on the blue Ford F-150 pickup truck. He settled behind the wheel, placing

Martha's muffins on the passenger seat. Before starting the engine, he checked his phone.

Two missed calls from Tessa. He dialed her back immediately.

She answered on the second ring. "Hey, big brother."

"Everything okay?"

"Yes, and no." Tessa sighed. "I haven't seen or heard from Cody in a couple of days."

Mitch pinched the bridge of his nose. "Did you try calling him?"

"Of course I called him. It went straight to voicemail. I'm not worried about his safety, Mitch. He can handle himself. I'm worried about..."

"What he might be doing," Mitch finished. Their brother had been home from his final deployment for a month. A full month of restless energy, midnight runs, solitary camping trips, and the kind of silence that spoke volumes about the things he wasn't saying.

"His truck was in the driveway went I left this morning, but his hiking pack wasn't by the back door. My guess is, he's up in the mountains somewhere."

"Probably," Mitch agreed, trying to ignore the memory of their mother's disappearances—first for hours, then days, before she left for good. "He needs space, Tess."

"I know that. But he also needs help, and he's too stubborn to ask for it." She paused. "Just like someone else I know."

"I'll talk to him." Mitch started the engine. "Earl mentioned seeing him out jogging on the ridge trail yesterday. He also said he could use help at the store."

"Work would be good for him. It would give him structure and purpose." Tessa's voice softened. "You doing okay? And don't give me the standard 'fine' answer. You sound tired."

Tessa was the only person who consistently asked how he was doing besides Martha—really asked, not the perfunctory greeting most people offered.

"I'm managing."

"Managing isn't living, Mitch."

"So I've been told." He watched as Leslie Williams propped open the door to her flower shop, arms full of bright summer blooms. "I've got patrol. I'll call if I hear from Cody."

"Okay." She hesitated. "I'll see you later. Love you, you know."

"Love you too, Tess. Try not to worry."

"Telling me not to worry is like telling the New River not to flow." She laughed softly. "Be safe."

The call ended, and Mitch pulled away from the curb, heading down Main Street at the unhurried pace of small-town law enforcement.

His route took him past Mountain Chic Boutique, its windows featuring summery displays that caught the morning light. The owner, Beth Rutledge, was arranging something inside, visible through the glass but focused on her task. Their paths crossed occasionally at community events or church, though they'd never spoken much beyond pleasantries. She'd been through a rough divorce last year—the kind of personal business that didn't stay private in a town like Laurel Ridge. He'd always admired the quiet dignity with which she'd rebuilt her life afterward.

His patrol continued through the residential streets, past Laurel Ridge Elementary, where his sister, Tessa, taught kindergarten, currently quiet for summer break. He checked the park, empty save for an early morning jogger, and then drove slowly past the Laurel Ridge Community Church, where preparations for Vacation Bible School were underway.

The radio remained blessedly silent. The tourist season brought its share of lost hikers, minor accidents, and the occasional rowdy visitor, but Monday mornings were typically quiet. Which meant it gave him too much time to think about Cody, about the restlessness that seemed to have followed him home after his Marine career.

Mitch understood that restlessness better than he'd admit. After raising his siblings, building a life defined by duty and service, he sometimes felt the boundaries of his existence pressing in like the walls of a room too small for its occupant. But unlike Cody, he'd learned to live with it, and to make peace with what life had handed him.

He turned onto the road that would take him out to check the campgrounds at the edge of town. The mountains rose around him, ancient and steadfast, a reminder of things that endured when people couldn't or wouldn't. His father had loved these mountains. "God's architecture," he'd called them, sturdy and reliable in a way human structures could never be.

God's architecture.

The phrase brought a smile to Mitch's face. His father's faith had been like that—uncomplicated, built on the foundation of believing in something bigger than himself. Mitch's own faith was more weathered, tested by loss and responsibility, but no less real for the wear it showed.

The campground was quiet, most of the tourists still enjoying their morning coffee or planning their day's adventures. He checked in with the ranger on duty, exchanged a few words about weather predictions and trail conditions, then continued his circuit of the town's perimeter.

By the time he pulled back onto Main Street, the day had fully bloomed. Multiple tourists wandered between shops, ice cream cones from Scoops Ice Cream Parlor already in hand, despite the early hour. Shopkeepers chatted on the sidewalks. Residents went about their business with the unhurried pace that had always defined Laurel Ridge.

He parked in front of the Sheriff's Department, a modest brick building that had served as his second home for the past twelve years. Inside, his new deputy, Lisa Waters, was at the front desk, phone tucked between ear and shoulder as she made notes.

"Yes, ma'am, I understand. We'll send someone to check on that noise complaint right away." She caught sight of Mitch and held up one finger. "Yes, ma'am. Thank you for calling." She hung up and shook her head. "Mrs. Patterson thinks the new family on Elm Street is playing their music too loud."

"Again?"

"Yep. I asked Reed to swing by, but I'm pretty sure it's just the kids practicing for the church talent show."

Mitch nodded. "Anything else I should know about?"

"Jason's handling a fender bender out by the grocery store. Nothing serious." She handed him a small stack of messages. "And Pastor Andrew called about the church meeting on Thursday."

"Thanks, Lisa." He took the messages and headed toward his office.

"Oh, and your brother stopped by looking for you about twenty minutes ago."

Mitch paused. "What did he say?"

"Said he'd catch you later. He didn't leave a message."

Relief and concern warred in his chest. "Thanks."

His office was exactly as he'd left it the night before—slightly unorganized, with stacks of reports to go through, and only one personal touch amidst the chaos. A framed photo of himself with Tessa and Cody at her college graduation. He settled behind his desk, flipping through the messages, but his mind was on his brother.

Cody had always been the wild one, even before the military—passionate, impulsive, charging headfirst into life while Mitch calculated risks and Tessa mediated between them. Their mother's abandonment had hit Cody the hardest, coming as it did during his formative teenage years. The military had given him structure, purpose, and brotherhood. Civilian life offered none of those things in such clear-cut terms.

A knock on his door interrupted his thoughts. Reed Dunbar stood there, hat in hand, his expression apologetic.

"Sorry to bother you, Sheriff, but the mayor's on line one. Something about the budget for the fall festival security."

Mitch nodded, reaching for the phone. "Thanks, Reed. Did you handle Mrs. Patterson's noise complaint?"

"Yes, sir. Just kids practicing 'This Little Light of Mine' on recorders. Not exactly Grammy material, but not worth a citation either."

"Appreciate it." Mitch said with a grin.

The rest of the morning passed in a blur of administrative tasks and phone calls. By noon, he was back in his patrol vehicle, heading out to the more remote areas of his jurisdiction. The radio kept him company, dispatch occasionally breaking in with updates that required minimal response.

As he drove the winding mountain roads, checking on the more isolated properties and keeping an eye out for his brother's familiar figure on the trails, Mitch found himself reflecting on the conversation with Tessa.

Managing isn't living. The words echoed uncomfortably accurate. When had he last done something purely for enjoyment? His life had become a series of responsibilities fulfilled and duties discharged. Even his home, the family farmhouse he'd maintained through sheer determination after his mother left, was more obligation than sanctuary.

The realization settled like a stone in his chest. At thirty-six, he'd built a life that revolved entirely around taking care of others. First his siblings, and now his community. Somewhere along the way, he'd forgotten how to want things for himself.

His radio crackled to life. "Sheriff, you copy?"

He reached for the handset. "Go ahead, dispatch."

"Got a call from out on Sunset Point. A couple of hikers reporting an injured man on the trail. Possible ankle sprain, nothing life-threatening, but they're requesting assistance."

"Copy that. I'm about ten minutes out. Send Reed as backup."

"Will do, Sheriff."

He flipped on his lights and increased his speed. As he navigated the familiar roads toward Sunset Point, he pushed aside his personal reflections.

Chapter 2

Beth Rutledge flipped the sign on the front door to "Open" precisely at ten o'clock, the way she had every Monday morning since opening Mountain Chic Boutique six years ago. She tucked a strand of blond hair behind her ear and scanned the store with a critical eye. The summer sundress collection needed a slight adjustment.

"Perfect is the enemy of done," she murmured, her grandmother's favorite saying. But she moved the dress's anyway, shifting them all to the right where sunlight from the front window kissed the fabric, highlighting their delicate eyelet patterns.

The store smelled of the cedar sachets she tucked between folded garments and the faint hint of the lemon cleaning spray she'd used on the countertops earlier. A classic jazz playlist provided a gentle background melody, creating the relaxed but sophisticated atmosphere she cultivated so carefully.

"Morning, boss!" Alisha Miller said as she entered the store, her dark curls bouncing with each step. "Sorry if I'm cutting it close. My car decided today was a good day to remind me I need new spark plugs."

"You're fine." Beth smiled at her store manager, the young woman's energy infectious. "I just opened up. Pearl called—said she'd be happy to pick up an extra shift today.... She'll be here at eleven."

"Good. That woman has more energy at sixty-two than I have at twenty-nine." Alisha dropped her purse beneath the counter and pulled out her phone. "I updated our social media last night with the new clothing arrivals. We already have twelve likes and three people asking about the blue maxi dress."

Beth nodded appreciatively. "I'm glad you take care of all that. Social media is not my thing."

Alisha laughed, the sound bouncing off the exposed brick walls. "That's why we're a good team. You've got the fashion sense and business brain, I've got the social media know how."

"And what do I have?" Pearl West's voice preceded her as she entered through the front door, a full hour before her shift. Her silver pixie cut framed a face lined with decades of laughter. "Besides being early, which my Harold always says is my worst quality. 'Pearl,' he says, 'you'd be early to your own funeral if they'd let you.'"

"You have the gift of making every customer feel like they've known you their whole life," Beth said. "What are you doing here so early?"

"I'm bored. Figured I might as well come make myself useful." Pearl surveyed the store with an approving nod. "That new scarf display is gorgeous!"

Leslie Williams swept in next, her arms laden with an arrangement of sunflowers and lavender sprigs in a blue ceramic vase. Her honey-blonde hair was piled atop her head in a messy bun that somehow looked intentional rather than haphazard.

"Good morning, gorgeous people of Mountain Chic!" Leslie announced, setting the vase on the counter. "I had extra sunflowers this morning and thought they belonged here. They match that yellow blouse in the window display."

"They're gorgeous," Beth said. "How much do I owe you?"

Leslie waved her off. "Friends and family discount. Which means they're free... but you can pay me in coffee and gossip later." She glanced around the store. "Where's that little notebook of yours? The one where you sketch your display ideas?"

"Back office. Why?"

"Because I have news." Leslie's eyes sparkled with the particular gleam that meant she was bursting with information. "The old toy store space... the one down on Cedar Street? I heard through the grapevine that Mr. Johnson might have found a renter."

Alisha perked up. "Really? It's been empty for, what, eight months?"

"Nearly a year," Beth corrected automatically, her mind already calculating. The toy store had closed when the owners retired to Florida, leaving a prime retail space vacant. She'd been eyeing it for months, wondering if the timing was right, or if she was ready.

Leslie's gaze fixed on Beth with a knowing intensity. "You should go look at it again. Today."

"I didn't say I was interested," Beth protested, but her voice lacked conviction.

"You didn't have to. Your face did the talking." Leslie grinned. "I know that look. It's your 'I'm calculating square footage and profit margins' look."

Pearl chuckled. "She's got you there, honey."

Beth sighed, but couldn't suppress her smile. "It's not that simple. Opening a second location is a huge risk. Especially now, with—" She stopped herself, unwilling to voice the worry that had been nagging at her. The summer tourist season had been great, but fall and winter were always leaner months.

"With what?" Leslie pressed.

"With the economy, supply chain issues, all of it." Beth moved to straighten a stack of folded summer cardigans. "Besides, Mountain Chic is just getting to where I want it. Adding a children's clothing store would mean starting over in many ways."

"Or it could mean doubling your customer base," Alisha pointed out, arranging a display of handcrafted jewelry. "Half the women who shop here complain they can't find cute clothes for their kids locally."

"That's actually why I came by," Leslie admitted. "Mrs. Henderson was in my shop yesterday ordering flowers for the church altar, and she mentioned her daughter's driving all the way to Charleston to get her granddaughter's back-to-school clothes. Said someone with 'Beth's eye for style' ought to open something for the younger set."

Beth's heart quickened despite her caution. A second store had been her dream. A store carrying cute children's clothing, with the same quality and style she prided herself on at Mountain Chic.

"I've been putting together some numbers," she admitted. "Just... hypothetically."

Leslie's eyebrows shot up. "Hypothetically, huh? Is that why you have a file folder labeled 'Mountain Chic Kid's' in your office? The one with paint chips and store layout sketches?"

"You were snooping in my office?"

"I was looking for a pen last week. The folder was right there on your desk and open, practically begging me to look." Leslie's expression softened. "Beth, you've wanted this for ages. At least go look at the space."

The store's front door opened again, and two women entered—tourists, Beth guessed from their unfamiliar faces and the way they scanned the boutique with eager curiosity.

"Welcome to Mountain Chic," Beth called warmly. "Please let us know if we can help you find anything special."

"I'll handle them," Alisha murmured. "You and Leslie go back to plotting retail domination."

Leslie took Beth's arm and guided her toward the back of the store. "Fifteen minutes. That's all I'm asking. Let's go look at the space during your lunch break."

"I need to do more research."

"Beth Catherine Rutledge, you have spreadsheets for your spreadsheets. You've researched this idea to death." Leslie's voice was gentle but firm. "Sometimes faith means taking the next step, even when you can't see the whole staircase."

"Are you quoting Martin Luther King Jr. to manipulate me?"

"Is it working?"

Beth laughed. "Maybe. I'll think about it."

"Good." Leslie squeezed her arm. "I've got to get back. Mrs. Tillman is coming in soon. She wants to order centerpieces for her granddaughter's baptism. But text me if you want to see that space later." She moved toward the door, pausing to call back, "Oh, and don't forget the town council meeting Wednesday night. They're discussing the fall festival budget."

"I'll be there," Beth promised, watching her friend leave in a whirlwind of energy, the same way she'd arrived.

***

Beth unwrapped the sandwich she'd packed that morning—turkey and avocado on whole wheat—and opened her laptop to check emails while she ate.

But her attention kept drifting to the folder on her desk. MOUN-TAIN CHIC KIDS, labeled in her precise handwriting. She pulled it toward her, flipping it open to reveal the sketches, notes, and paint chips she'd been collecting for months.

The children's clothing store had been more than a passing thought. It had been her secret project, something to focus on during the lonely evenings after her divorce, when the silence in her house threatened to swallow her whole. She'd thrown herself into research, designing a second retail space that would complement Mountain Chic while standing on its own.

But every time she got close to taking a concrete step, something held her back. Fear, she recognized now. Fear of overextending herself. Fear of failure. Fear of trusting her instincts.

Beth leaned back in her chair as an unwelcome memory washed over her.

"I can't do this anymore, Beth."

Matt's words had cut through the quiet kitchen that evening over a year ago, slicing into her with surgical precision. He'd stood there, suitcases already packed and car keys in hand.

"What do you mean, you can't do this?" She'd been chopping vegetables for dinner. "Do what, exactly?"

"This." He'd gestured vaguely around them. "Small-town life. The routine. The... predictability of it all. I'm bored."

She'd set the knife down carefully and turned to him. "I'm not following."

"I've met someone. In Charleston. She's... exciting. Fun. Different."

Different from her.

Exciting, unlike her.

Fun, unlike her.

"Excuse me?" she'd asked, her voice surprisingly steady.

"I didn't plan it, Beth. It just happened."

Affairs didn't "just happen," she'd wanted to scream. They were choices, one small betrayal after another.

"Is she why you've been 'working late' so often?" The pieces had fallen into place with sickening clarity. The late nights. The extended business trips that had seemed unnecessary. The growing distance she'd attributed to stress.

He'd nodded, and something in her had broken.

"I never meant to hurt you," he'd said, the platitude so inadequate it had almost been laughable.

"Get out." The words had tasted like ashes in her mouth.

And he had. Just like that. Eight years of marriage ended in a ten-minute conversation, followed by the sound of his car driving away.

Beth shook herself back to the present. Her sandwich sat untouched on her desk, her appetite gone. Outside her office, she could hear the gentle hum of the boutique. Alisha's laugh, Pearl's voice warm with customer service charm and the soft music playing overhead.

Mountain Chic had been her refuge after Matt left. She'd poured every ounce of hurt and anger into making it even more successful, proving to herself that she didn't need him. That she could continue to build something beautiful and successful on her own.

And she had. The boutique was thriving. She was respected in the community, financially stable, and healing from Matt's betrayal.

So why did the thought of starting a second store fill her with such trepidation?

Trust. That was the crux of it. Matt's betrayal had shattered her trust—not just in him, but in her own judgment. If she could be so wrong about the man she'd married, how could she trust herself with bigger decisions?

She unwrapped her sandwich and took a bite, forcing herself to eat despite her lack of appetite. As she chewed, her gaze drifted to the small framed quote on her desk, a gift from Leslie after the divorce: "Sometimes God calms the storm. Sometimes He lets the storm rage and calms His child."

The words had been a comfort during the worst days of her pain. Perhaps those words were meant for this moment, too.

Her phone pinged with a text from Leslie: Meet me at the old toy store space at 1:00.

Beth smiled. Leslie's gentle pushing was undoubtedly what she sometimes needed—a counterbalance to her caution.

She texted back before she could talk herself out of it: I'll be there. Just to look.

Chapter 3

The silver pendant necklace was gone.

Beth blinked, then checked again, her fingers trailing over the blue velvet display where three necklaces should have been arranged in a graceful arc. Only two remained. She distinctly remembered positioning the silver teardrop pendant with the small mountain etching—one of her favorite pieces from a local artisan—front and center yesterday afternoon, and didn't recall it showing as sold on her end of the day reports from yesterday.

"That's odd," she murmured, glancing around as if the necklace might have somehow migrated to another display. The boutique was quiet, not yet open for customers. The only sounds were the soft click of hangers as Alisha arranged a new shipment of summer blouses and the gentle whir of the ceiling fan overhead.

Beth moved to the adjacent jewelry cabinet, an open style display case near the register. Her breath caught as she scanned the contents. The turquoise beaded bracelet set—a trio of delicate strands with silver moon charms—was also missing. She distinctly remembered helping a customer try it on yesterday, but the woman had ultimately decided on a different style. These pieces hadn't shown as sold in yesterday's reports, either.

"Alisha?" Beth kept her voice casual, despite the fluttering in her chest. "Did we sell the silver mountain pendant necklace yesterday? The one from Riverview Designs?"

Alisha looked up from the clothing rack, her brow furrowed. "No, I don't think so. The only jewelry I sold yesterday was those pearl earrings to Mrs. Lawrence and a beaded bracelet to another customer." She approached the display, peering over Beth's shoulder. "It's not there?"

"No. And neither is the turquoise bracelet set that was in this case." Beth tapped the glass where an empty space sat between two similar items.

"That's weird. Maybe Pearl sold them?"

"They weren't listed as sold in yesterday's reports."

A chill spread through her as she moved methodically through the store, checking other displays. A pair of sterling silver earrings with tiny blue stones—missing. A handcrafted leather cuff bracelet—gone. All small items, easily pocketed.

"I need to double-check the inventory records," Beth said, heading toward her office with quick, purposeful steps.

Her laptop hummed to life. She opened the inventory spreadsheet, which synced automatically with her POS system. Every time a piece rang up at the register, the sheet stamped the sale time and adjusted the stock count. Yet, according to the records, the missing items had never been sold at all.

Could the software have made a mistake? She thought to herself. But deep down, she knew her inventory management was flawless.

Alisha appeared in the doorway. "Beth, I found another empty spot. Those hand-painted wooden bangles that were in the corner display? Three of them are gone... they aren't showing as sold on the end of the day report, either."

Beth pressed her fingers against her temples. "Shoplifting. How is this possible? We've never had a problem before."

"Maybe it happened during that rush yesterday afternoon? When those three women came in together and were trying on practically everything in the store?"

The memory came back clearly—a trio of tourists, enthusiastic and chatty, moving throughout the boutique while she, Pearl, and Alisha helped them find sizes and styles. It had been busy, their attention divided.

"I need to call the Sheriff's office," Beth said, her voice steadier than she felt. The violation settled over her like an unwelcome shawl—heavy and suffocating.

Alisha nodded. "I'll finish setting up out front. We open in twenty minutes."

Beth reached for the phone, then paused. Would calling the police do any good? The thief or thieves are probably long gone now. The missing items weren't extremely expensive—around five hundred dollars' worth in total.

She scrolled through her contact list on her cell phone, looking for the non-emergency number for the Sheriff's department, which she'd programmed into her phone years ago but had never needed to use.

"Laurel Ridge Sheriff's Department, Deputy Dunbar speaking."

"Hi, Reed. This is Beth Rutledge at Mountain Chic Boutique. I need to report some stolen merchandise."

"Mornin', Beth." Reed's voice was professional, but kind. "Can you tell me what happened?"

She explained the situation, describing each missing item, and when she believed the theft had occurred.

"Alright, I've got all that down," Reed said when she finished. "I'll send someone over to take a formal report. Do you have security cameras in the store?"

"No." The admission made her feel foolish. "I never thought... this is Laurel Ridge. Nothing like this has ever happened in my store before."

"It happens, even in small towns." There was a pause, some muffled conversation in the background. "Actually, Sheriff Baker is available right now. He'll be heading your way in about fifteen minutes, if that works for you?"

A flicker of surprise ran through her. The Sheriff himself? For a few pieces of stolen jewelry?

"That's fine," she managed. "I'll be here."

After hanging up, Beth walked to the small bathroom attached to her office. She splashed cool water on her face, taking deep breaths. In the mirror, her reflection showed a woman trying very hard to appear unruffled. Her blonde hair was neatly styled, her blue blouse unwrinkled, but her eyes betrayed her—wide with a mixture of anger and unease.

This is just a bump in the road. Things get stolen from stores every day. It doesn't mean anything.

Yet, it did mean something: someone with sticky fingers had violated her space. Her sense of peace and security, something that she'd worked so hard to build, felt cracked now.

Beth heard Pearl's cheerful greeting to Alisha toward the front of the store as she arrived for her shift. Beth straightened her shoulders and went out to meet her.

"Morning, honey!" Pearl called, then stopped short when she saw Beth's face. "What's wrong? You look like you've seen a ghost."

Alisha briefly explained the situation while Beth flipped the sign on the door to "Open."

"Well, I never," Pearl declared, indignation coloring her voice. "Who would do such a thing? What is this world coming to?"

"The Sheriff is coming to take a report," Beth said, moving behind the counter to straighten items that didn't need straightening. "Let's just try to have a normal day, okay?"

But "normal" felt impossible as she moved through the motions of opening procedures, checking emails, and greeting the first customers of the day. Every time the door opened, she glanced up, expecting to see Sheriff Baker's tall, sturdy frame.

Chapter 4

Mitch pulled his patrol truck to a stop in front of Mountain Chic Boutique, killing the engine while observing the store's elegant window display. He took an extra moment to gather his thoughts, reviewing what Deputy Dunbar had told him about the theft report. A few pieces of jewelry missing—not exactly a major crime in the grand scheme of things, but in Laurel Ridge, even small violations deserved serious attention.

His gaze drifted to his reflection in the rearview mirror. He straightened his uniform collar and ran a hand through his hair where his hat had ruffled it.

The weight of his duty belt felt familiar against his hip as he stepped onto the sidewalk. A tone chimed pleasantly when he pushed open the boutique's door, announcing his arrival. The store's interior hit his senses all at once—soft music playing from hidden speakers, the subtle scent of something floral but not overpowering, and lighting that somehow made everything look more vibrant.

"Good morning, Sheriff!" Pearl called from behind the register, where she was helping a customer. "Beth's expecting you. She's over there."

Mitch nodded his thanks, turning in the direction Pearl pointed. Beth glanced up from the scarves she was arranging as he approached, her hazel-green eyes meeting his.

He'd seen Beth around town plenty of times over the years. They attended the same church, crossed paths at community events, and exchanged pleasantries when appropriate. But something about seeing her here, in her element, struck him differently. The morning light from the front windows caught in her blonde hair, giving it a warmth that complemented her blue blouse.

"Sheriff Baker," she said, extending her hand. "Thank you for coming so quickly."

Her handshake was firm and professional. A business owner who knew her worth.

"Ms. Rutledge," he replied, trying to ignore how his hand seemed to register every detail of hers—the softness of her palm and tiny delicate fingers. "I understand you've had some items go missing."

She nodded, pulling her hand back. "Yes. Would you like to talk in my office? I've made a list of everything that seems to have walked away."

"Lead the way."

He followed her through the store, to her office, which was smaller than he'd expected, but organized with the same attention to detail evident in the store displays. A desk sat in the middle of the room. Built-in shelving held fabric samples, catalogs, and neatly labeled folders. A mood board hung on another wall, featuring swatches of color and magazine clippings that probably represented future displays or merchandise ideas.

"Please, have a seat," she said, gesturing to the chair across from her desk.

He settled into it, removing his hat and placing it on his knee. "Why don't you tell me exactly what happened, starting with when you first noticed things were missing?"

Beth sat down, her posture straight. "I came in this morning around eight-thirty. I always do a walk-through of the store before we open at ten, checking displays, straightening merchandise, that sort of thing. Then I noticed the silver pendant necklace was missing from the display near the register."

She slid a piece of paper across the desk. "Once I realized that was gone, I did a more thorough check and found these other items missing as well. Nothing extremely valuable on its own, but altogether..." she trailed off, frustration evident in the slight furrow of her brow.

Mitch scanned the list: the silver pendant necklace, a turquoise bracelet set, sterling silver earrings with blue stones, a leather cuff bracelet, and wooden bangles. Approximately $500 worth of merchandise.

"And you're sure these items are missing??" he asked, meeting her eyes again.

"I triple-checked our sales records. These items just... vanished."

"Do you have any idea when this might have happened?"

"Yesterday afternoon seems most likely. We had a rush around two o'clock—three women came in together, trying on clothes and accessories. Pearl, Alisha and I were each helping them, and moving around throughout the store. It would have been easy for someone to pocket small items while we were distracted." She paused. "I feel so stupid for not being more vigilant."

Her self-recrimination stirred something protective in him. "This isn't your fault, Ms. Rutledge."

"Beth, please."

"Beth," he amended, surprised at how naturally her name came to his lips. "Most businesses deal with theft at some point. Even in small towns like ours."

She nodded, though the tension in her shoulders remained. "I just never thought... It feels like a violation, you know... like some evil being crossed into my personal space?"

He did know. He'd seen that same reaction countless times—the shock when someone realized that the safety they'd taken for granted had cracks in it.

"I'll need to ask a few more questions about your security measures," he said, pulling out his notebook. "Do you have cameras in the store?"

"No." A flush of embarrassment colored her cheeks. "It never seemed necessary until now."

"How many employees do you have?"

"Just three of us. Myself, Alisha Miller, and Pearl West. We're all here now."

"And yesterday?"

"The three of us were here as well."

Mitch made a note, his pen scratching against the paper. "How do you secure the store at closing?"

"Standard deadbolt on the front door, and another on the back entrance. The display windows have security film on them—they won't shatter easily. And the jewelry cases are locked at night, but during business hours they stay open for customers to try things on."

As Beth continued explaining her security procedures, Mitch found his attention divided. Part of him—the professional sheriff—was cataloging the information, already thinking about potential leads and prevention strategies. But another part was noticing the way her hands moved expressively as she spoke, the slight raspiness in her voice, and the determination that animated her features even as she described something upsetting.

"Sheriff? Did you hear my question?"

Mitch blinked, realizing he'd missed something. "I'm sorry, could you repeat that?"

She tilted her head slightly. "I asked if there were any other shoplifting reports among businesses in town lately."

"Not that I'm aware of," he replied, inwardly chastising himself for the lapse in attention. "This is the first shoplifting report we've had this month. The last one was at Talbot's General Store, but that was kids taking candy bars. Nothing organized or valuable."

The door to the office opened, and a young woman with dark wavy hair poked her head in. "Sorry to interrupt, but Mrs. Holloway is asking about that special order jacket, Beth. I can't remember where you said you put it."

"Bottom shelf under the cash register. The garment bag has her name on it."

"Thanks," the woman said, her gaze shifting curiously to Mitch before she retreated.

Beth smiled apologetically. "That's Alisha, my assistant manager."

"I'd like to speak with her if that's all right. She was working yesterday, right?"

"Yes, and she was here when I discovered the missing items this morning as well."

Mitch nodded, jotting another note. When he looked up, he found Beth watching him with an intensity that made him unexpectedly self-conscious.

"What?" he asked.

"Nothing, just..." She shook her head slightly. "I've never seen you in sheriff mode. You're very thorough."

"Just doing my job," he replied, unsure how to take her observation.

"Well, I appreciate it. Most people would probably think a few missing pieces of jewelry aren't worth this level of attention."

"Most crimes in Laurel Ridge are small," he said. "Doesn't make them any less important to the people affected."

Something in her expression softened. Mitch became acutely aware of how small her office was, and how the scent of her perfume—something light with hints of vanilla and distinctly feminine—mingled in the office space.

He cleared his throat, looking back down at his notes. "I'd like to see the areas where the items were displayed, if you wouldn't mind showing me."

"Of course." She stood up, smoothing her slacks. "Follow me."

They returned to the main floor, where Beth guided him to each display area, describing exactly how the missing items had been arranged. He watched her small hands as she demonstrated, noting how they moved with precision and care.

The knowledge of her personal history floated at the edges of his awareness—not from any official reports, but from the inevitable small-town whispers that had circulated when her husband left. Mitch had never been one for gossip, but he remembered thinking at the time that any man who would abandon a woman like Beth Rutledge must be a fool.

"This is where the silver pendant was," she was saying, indicating a blue velvet display near the register. "It was right here, between these two necklaces. The design was distinctive—a teardrop shape with a small etched mountain scene. One of our most popular pieces."

Mitch studied the display, then the surrounding area. "Is there always someone stationed at the register?"

"During business hours, quite often. But during that rush yesterday, each of us was helping customers throughout the store."

"And the turquoise bracelets?"

She moved to a glass case a few feet away. "Here."

As she continued showing him the locations, Mitch made mental notes about sight lines, store layout, and potential blind spots. The boutique was well-designed for displaying merchandise, but not necessarily for preventing theft. Too many small, valuable items within easy reach.

"What security measures have you been considering?" he asked when she'd shown him all the relevant areas.

Beth crossed her arms, a defensive posture he'd observed in many people when feeling vulnerable. "I haven't had an opportunity to research options yet. This just happened."

"I'd recommend cameras at a minimum," he said, keeping his tone conversational rather than authoritative. "At least covering the register area and jewelry displays. And possibly a silent alarm system that connects directly to your cell phone that could alert you of activity in certain areas."

"That sounds expensive."

"It can be," he acknowledged. "But there are scalable options for small businesses. I can put you in touch with the company that installed the system at the bank. They're reliable and fair with pricing."

Her expression shifted, almost imperceptibly, toward defensiveness. "I appreciate the suggestion, but I need to consider what makes financial sense for my business."

"Of course," he said, sensing he'd somehow overstepped. "It's just a recommendation."

Beth's shoulders relaxed slightly. "I know. I'm sorry if I sound prickly. This whole situation has me on edge. It's really upset me."

"Understandable."

Alisha approached them, having finished with her customer. "Beth, do you need me for anything? Pearl's handling the register."

"Actually," Mitch said, "I'd like to ask you a few questions about yesterday, if you have a moment."

"Sure," Alisha replied, glancing at Beth, who nodded her approval.

"Can you walk me through yesterday afternoon? Specifically, around the time you had three female customers in the store that occupied yourself, Pearl and Beth?"

Alisha described the scene—three women who'd come in together, spread out through the boutique, trying on clothes and accessories, asking questions that required herself, Pearl and Beth to move in various areas around the store.

"Did any of them seem suspicious to you?" Mitch asked. "Anyone else lingering near the jewelry displays or asking questions that might have been meant to distract you?"

Alisha frowned thoughtfully. "Not really. Everyone who was here during that time all bought something. The three women in particular bought a sundress, a scarf, and a pair of earrings. The women were chatty, but not in a way that seemed off."

"Do you remember their names or anything distinctive about them?"

"The credit card receipts would have names," Beth interjected. "I can pull those for you."

"That would be helpful," Mitch said.

As Beth went to retrieve the information, Alisha leaned closer to Mitch. "She's taking this pretty hard," she said in a low voice. "Beth puts everything she's got into this place. It's not just a store for her."

"I understand," Mitch replied, his gaze following Beth as she moved behind the counter.

Alisha studied him with unexpected shrewdness. "You know, Sheriff, I don't think I've ever seen you in here before today."

"I've never had a reason to be in this store before today... just doing my job," he said.

Beth returned with several receipts. "These are all the transactions from yesterday afternoon between one and four. The three women Alisha mentioned were probably these sequential purchases around 2:30."

Mitch took the receipts, noting the names: Jennifer Morris, Stephanie Keller, and Amy Prescott. All with credit cards issued from banks outside their county.

"Tourists, most likely, I don't recognize the names," he said.

"Yes, I remember them mentioning they were staying at the Mountain View B&B."

He jotted their names down in his notebook. "I'll follow up with them. They might have noticed something even if they weren't involved."

Beth tucked a strand of hair behind her ear, the simple gesture drawing his attention to the graceful line of her neck.

"I should let you get back to your customers," he said.

"Right." She nodded, but didn't immediately move away. "What happens next? With the investigation, I mean."

"I'll file the report and follow up with these leads," he said. "We'll check with other businesses downtown, see if anyone else has experienced similar thefts."

"And meanwhile?"

"In the meantime... I'd recommend being extra vigilant. Maybe adjust how you display the more valuable items, keep them where they can be easily monitored."

"I'll move the jewelry displays closer to the register for now," she said.

"Good thinking. And I'll have our patrols make regular passes by your store for the next few weeks, especially at opening and closing time."

A hint of resistance flashed in her eyes. "I appreciate that, Sheriff, but I don't need special treatment. I'm perfectly capable of handling myself and my store."

There was a story behind that reaction—something deeper than simple independence. Mitch had interviewed enough people over the years to recognize when someone had been deeply hurt or affected by something in their past.

"It's not special treatment," he said carefully. "It's what we'd do for any business that's reported theft."

Her expression softened. "Of course. I'm sorry. Like I said earlier, this has me rattled."

"Perfectly normal reaction," he assured her. "I'll head back to the station and get this process started. If you notice anything else missing or remember any additional details, don't hesitate to call."

"I will. Thank you for coming so quickly."

As he turned to leave, Pearl appeared with a small paper bag. "Sheriff, take these with you," she said, pressing the bag into his hands. "Chocolate chip cookies. I baked them this morning. A little thank you for looking out for our Beth."

"Oh, Pearl, stop," Beth protested, her cheeks coloring. "The Sheriff is just doing his job."

"And doing it well," Pearl insisted. "My Harold always says you can tell a man's character by how he treats the small problems, not just the big ones."

Mitch accepted the cookies with a smile. "Thank you, ma'am. Tell Harold hello for me."

"I'll do that," Pearl said with a wink. "Now, you make sure you keep an eye on our girl here. She works too hard to have people stealing from her."

"Pearl!" Beth's embarrassment deepened.

"What? It's true." The older woman patted Beth's arm affectionately before returning to her customer.

Mitch met Beth's eyes one final time. "I'll be in touch soon with any updates."

She nodded. "Thank you, Sheriff."

As he left, the summer heat hit him like a physical force after the cool interior of the boutique. He paused on the sidewalk, looking back through the display window. Beth had already returned to helping a customer, her smile warm and engaging as she held up a blouse for the woman to consider.

Inside his truck, Mitch sat for a moment without starting the engine, the cookie bag on the passenger seat next to him.

Beth Rutledge.

He'd noticed in the past that she was a beautiful woman. But today, watching her in her element, seeing the passion she had for her business and the dignified way she handled the violation of her space—affected him in a way he couldn't define.

His phone buzzed with a text from Deputy Dunbar: Mrs. Patterson called again about the noise. Want me to handle it?

The message yanked him back to reality. He was the sheriff, not some teenager with a crush. Whatever he'd felt in that boutique needed to be packed away, filed under "inappropriate" and forgotten.

He texted back: I'll take care of it.

As he pulled away from Mountain Chic, Mitch glanced in his rearview mirror one last time. He would investigate the theft with the same thoroughness he applied to every case in Laurel Ridge. He would follow up on leads, check with the B&B about the tourists, and ensure extra patrols passed by her store.

But he would do it all with the professional distance required of his position. Whatever personal interest he might feel would remain exactly that—personal, private, and unacted upon.

At least, that was the plan as he turned the corner, Beth's boutique disappearing from view.

Chapter 5

Mitch pushed open the door to Martha's Diner. The lunch rush had mostly cleared out, leaving only a handful of patrons scattered among the red vinyl booths. He hadn't planned on stopping for lunch—his schedule was already packed with meetings and patrols—but the text from Martha ("Just pulled fresh biscuits out of the oven. Better hurry before they're gone.") had proved too tempting to resist.

His gaze swept the diner out of habit, a lawman's instinct to assess his surroundings. That's when he spotted her—Beth Rutledge, sitting in a corner booth with Leslie Williams from the flower shop. Beth's blonde hair caught the light from the window, and she was gesturing animatedly as she spoke, more relaxed than he'd seen her yesterday when taking the theft report.

Martha appeared from behind the counter, coffeepot in hand. "Well, look who decided to grace us with his presence. Almost thought I'd have to eat those biscuits myself."

"Never doubt my dedication to your cooking, Martha," Mitch replied, returning her smile.

"You want a booth today or your usual seat at the counter?"

Before Mitch could respond, Beth looked up and noticed him. Their eyes met across the diner, and she offered a small, tentative smile of recognition. She said something to Leslie, who turned his way and waved him over with enthusiastic gestures.

"Looks like you've got options," Martha commented with a knowing glance between him and Beth's table.

Mitch hesitated for just a moment. His relationship with Beth Rutledge up to this point had been occasional nods at church, brief exchanges at community events, and yesterday's theft report. Joining her for lunch felt like crossing some invisible line.

But Leslie was already scooting over in the booth, making room. "Sheriff! Perfect timing. We were just debating whether Beth should call you about some security options for her store."

Beth's cheeks flushed slightly. "We were not. Leslie's exaggerating. You're welcome to join us if you'd like. Unless you're on official business?"

"Just grabbing lunch," Mitch said, finding himself oddly grateful for the invitation. "If you're sure I'm not interrupting?"

"Not at all," Beth said. "Please, join us."

As Mitch settled into the booth, Martha appeared with his coffee. "Coffee Sheriff?"

"Please." He nodded, then turned to Beth. "I was actually going to stop by your store today. I've checked with other businesses in town. No one else has noticed any missing merchandise, which might suggest yours was an isolated incident."

Beth nodded. "That's good to hear, I think. Though I'm not sure if it's better or worse to be singled out."

"Either way, I'm taking it seriously," Mitch assured her. "Deputy Waters is reaching out to neighboring towns to see if they've had similar incidents, and she's visiting pawn shops around the area looking for your stolen merchandise."

Leslie leaned forward, curiosity brightening her eyes. "Do you think it was tourists? Not locals?"

Mitch considered his answer carefully. "Most theft is opportunistic. Summer brings more strangers to our town for sure, which means more opportunities for them as well as locals. But it's too early to make assumptions."

Martha returned with his plate—country-fried steak with gravy, green beans, and two biscuits that made his mouth water just looking at them. She set it down with a flourish, then turned to Beth and Leslie. "Can I get you ladies anything else?"

"I'm fine, thank you," Beth said, gesturing to her half-eaten salad.

"Maybe just the check when you get a chance," Leslie added.

After Martha left, an awkward silence settled over the table. Mitch wasn't known for his conversational skills, and Beth seemed equally uncertain how to proceed beyond the professional discussion.

Leslie, however, had no such reservations. "So, Sheriff, what do you think about the plans for the fall festival? I heard the budget committee is considering cutting the hay ride this year."

"First, I've heard of it," Mitch replied, cutting into his steak. "But budget meetings aren't exactly my favorite part of serving on the town council."

"You're on the council?" Beth asked, looking genuinely interested.

"Going on five years now. Mostly handle public safety concerns." He shrugged. "Honestly, I'd rather be on patrol than sitting through another three-hour debate about streetlamp replacements."

Beth's lips curved into a small smile. "I can imagine. I attended one meeting about the Christmas decoration budget last year, and I thought I might never escape."

"Dorothy Henderson can talk about garland specifications for forty-five minutes without taking a breath," Mitch agreed.

Beth laughed—a genuine sound that brightened her entire face. "And don't get her started on the proper way to wrap the lights around the gazebo. I think she actually brought diagrams last year."

"Blueprints," Mitch corrected, finding himself smiling. "With color-coding and numbered instructions."

Leslie looked between them with undisguised interest. "Well, well. Who knew the Sheriff had a sense of humor hiding under that badge?"

Mitch's phone vibrated against his hip. He pulled it out to check the screen and found a text from Cody: "Took that job with Earl. Starting tomorrow."

Relief mingled with cautious hope in Mitch's chest. Earl's offer had been genuine, but he hadn't been sure Cody would accept it. His brother's adjustment to civilian life had been rocky at best, his restlessness a constant concern.

"Everything okay?" Beth asked, her voice gentle with concern.

Mitch looked up. "Yes, sorry. Just a message from my brother. He's taken a job with Earl at the hardware store."

"That's good news, isn't it?" Leslie asked.

"It is," Mitch confirmed, tucking his phone away. "Cody's been back from the Marines for a month now. His adjustment back here at home has been... challenging."

Beth nodded, understanding in her eyes. "I can only imagine. The structure must be so different from military life."

"I think that's part of it," Mitch said. "The military gives a person purpose, routine, and clear expectations. Civilian life is more... open-ended."

"Sometimes too many choices can be overwhelming for some people," Beth said.

"My father always said the hardest part of coming home from Vietnam wasn't what he'd seen there, but finding his place here again," Leslie offered. "He said people expected him to just slot back into his old life, but he was different, and home was different too."

Mitch nodded, appreciating her perspective. "Cody's struggling with that exact thing. He's changed, but everyone here still sees him as the kid who left twelve years ago."

"Including you?" Beth asked.

The question made Mitch pause. Did he still see Cody as his little brother, the one he'd raised after their mother left? The one who needed protection and guidance?

"Sometimes," he admitted. "It's challenging to stop being the responsible one when that's been your role for so long."

"I understand that," Beth said, her gaze steady on his. "Old habits can be hard to break."

There was something in her words that suggested personal experience—perhaps related to her divorce, though Mitch would never ask directly. Laurel Ridge was small enough that he knew the basic facts: her husband had left her over a year ago, filed for divorce, and moved to Charleston with another woman. The gossip mill around Laurel Ridge had filled in the details.

"Speaking of habits," Leslie interjected with a glance at her watch, "I should get back to the shop. My delivery from the Greenbrier nursery is coming this afternoon." She nudged Beth with her elbow. "You coming?"

Beth hesitated, glancing between Leslie and Mitch. "Actually, I think I'll finish my coffee, if you don't mind heading back without me."

"Sure thing. I'll see you later." She slid out of the booth, gathering her purse. "Sheriff, always a pleasure."

"Likewise," Mitch replied, standing briefly as Leslie departed, a habit his father had ingrained in him from childhood.

As Mitch sat back down, it hit him that he was now alone with Beth. The professional pretext of their conversation had largely evaporated, leaving them in uncharted territory.

"So," Beth said, wrapping her hands around her coffee mug, "is Earl's Hardware a good place for your brother to work?"

"I think so," Mitch replied, grateful for the easy topic. "Earl's patient and understands more than most about readjustment. His son served in Desert Storm."

Beth nodded. "That makes sense. Support from someone who gets it, even indirectly, can make all the difference."

"What about you?" Mitch asked before he could reconsider the question. "I heard through the grapevine that you were looking at a vacant store space the other day?"

Beth's expression brightened. "The old toy store on Cedar Street. I've been considering opening a second store that offers children's clothing."

"That would probably be a good business move," Mitch said, genuinely impressed. "The closest dedicated children's clothing store is in Charleston, isn't it?"

She nodded. "Parents are always asking if I'll start carrying things for their kids." She traced the rim of her mug with one finger, her expression turning thoughtful. "It's a big step, though. More risk, and more responsibility."

"But potentially rewarding."

"Yes," she agreed, looking up at him. "I keep going back and forth with my decision. One store already keeps me busy enough."

"From what I saw yesterday, you run a tight ship at Mountain Chic," Mitch said. "The inventory system you described to me on Monday sounded impressive."

Beth smiled, a hint of pride warming her expression. "Thank you. I'm a bit of a control freak when it comes to the store. Everything in its place, everything accounted for."

"That's probably why the theft bothered you so much," Mitch observed. "Beyond the obvious reasons."

Her smile faded slightly. "You're right." She paused, studying him. "You're very perceptive, Sheriff."

"Mitch," he reminded her. "And it's part of the job—reading people, and understanding what's not being said."

"Is that why you became a sheriff? Because you're good at reading people?"

"Partly," Mitch admitted, considering his answer. Few people asked him about his career choice; most in Laurel Ridge simply accepted that Mitch Baker was the sheriff, as if he'd been born to the role. "But mostly I wanted to protect people. Keep them safe."

"Like you did with your siblings," Beth said, then looked embarrassed. "I'm sorry. That was presumptuous. Small-town gossip—I've heard you raised your brother and sister after your mother left."

"It's not gossip if it's true. And yes, that experience definitely shaped my career choice."

Beth nodded, understanding in her eyes. "Life has a way of doing that—setting us on paths we might not have chosen deliberately, but that somehow fit who we need to become."

"That's an insightful way of looking at it."

"Not original to me," Beth admitted with a small smile. "Pastor Andrew said something similar during counseling after my divorce."

Mitch nodded. "Before Reverend Eli retired, his counseling helped me through some rough patches, too. After my father died, and again when my mother left. Paster Andrew and I have spoken a lot lately as well. He has a gift for helping people find their footing when the ground shifts underneath them."

"Yes, he does," Beth agreed. "He helped me see that even painful experiences can shape us in necessary ways, if we let them."

Mitch found himself wondering how her divorce had shaped her—what strengths it had forged, and what vulnerabilities it had exposed. In their brief interactions, he'd seen both her careful control and her underlying resilience.

"I should probably get back to the station," Mitch said, glancing at his watch. He'd already stayed longer than he'd planned, drawn into conversation more easily than usual.

"Of course," Beth said, reaching for her purse. "I need to get back to the boutique as well."

Mitch signaled to Martha for the check, but she waved him off. "On the house today, Sheriff. You've been working too hard lately."

"Martha—" he began to protest.

"Don't 'Martha' me," she interrupted with a mock stern expression. "Consider it payment for keeping our town safe."

Mitch sighed, but nodded his thanks. Martha's generosity was as stubborn as it was genuine.

As they both stood to leave, Beth hesitated. "Thank you for taking the theft at my store seriously. I know it must seem minor compared to other issues you deal with."

"No crime is minor when it affects someone's sense of security," Mitch said firmly. "That's something I learned early in this job. What matters isn't always the monetary value, but the impact."

Beth studied him for a moment, as if seeing something new. "Well, thank you all the same."

They walked to the door together, Mitch automatically holding it open for her.

"I'll keep you updated if we learn anything about the theft," Mitch said as they stepped onto the sidewalk.

"I appreciate that." Beth squinted against the sunlight, adjusting her purse strap on her shoulder.

A moment of awkward silence stretched between them, neither quite sure how to end an encounter that had started professionally but shifted into something more personal.

"Good luck with your expansion plans," Mitch finally said. "A children's store would be a great addition to Laurel Ridge."

Beth's smile returned, genuine and warm. "Thank you. I haven't decided for sure yet, but I'm leaning that way."

"Sometimes you just have to take the leap. Even when you can't see exactly where you'll land."

"My grandmother used to say something similar," Beth replied. "'Faith is taking the first step without seeing the whole staircase.'"

"Smart woman, your grandmother."

"She was," Beth agreed, a fond expression crossing her face. "Well, I should go. Thank you again."

"Anytime," Mitch said, and was surprised to realize he meant it.

He watched her walk toward Mountain Chic, her steps purposeful but unhurried. There was something about Beth Rutledge that intrigued him—a complexity beneath her polished exterior that he hadn't expected.

His phone vibrated again, this time with a call from the station. Duty called, as it always did. But as Mitch headed back toward his patrol vehicle, he found himself replaying his conversation with Beth, turning her insights over in his mind.

Beth Rutledge was more than the successful boutique owner he'd categorized her as—she was perceptive, thoughtful, and carrying her burdens with quiet grace. For the first time in years, Mitch found himself curious about someone in a way that had nothing to do with his badge or his responsibilities.

As he started the engine, he glanced once more toward Mountain Chic, where Beth had just disappeared through the front door.

Chapter 6

itch was halfway up the steps to Mountain Chic when the raised voices inside stopped him short. Through the storefront window, he spotted Beth standing behind the counter, her posture straight but not rigid, facing a red-faced man who leaned aggressively across the glass display case.

"—don't care what your policy says! I paid good money and I want my refund!" The man's voice carried clearly through the door, his finger jabbing toward Beth with each word.

Mitch's protective instincts flared immediately. He pushed open the door, the cheerful bell announcing his entrance in stark contrast to the tension filling the boutique. Beth's eyes flicked briefly to him, registering his presence, before returning to the agitated customer.

"Sir, as I've explained, I can't accept returns on sale merchandise after fourteen days," Beth said, her voice steady and professional. "According to your receipt, you purchased this three weeks ago."

"That's highway robbery!" The man slapped his palm against the counter. A small stack of business cards toppled over. "My wife never even wore this!"

Pearl and Alisha hovered nearby, tension visible in their expressions as they tried to appear busy helping other customers while keeping watchful eyes on the situation.

Mitch moved quietly to the side, not interfering but making his presence known. His uniform alone often defused situations, but he was interested in seeing how Beth would handle this.

"I understand your frustration, Mr. Collins," Beth said, smoothing the shirt in question with careful hands. "While I can't offer a refund, I'd be happy to exchange it for store credit. We just received some new items your wife might love."

Mr. Collins huffed, his shoulders still tight with anger. "That's not good enough. Do you know how far we drove to get here? My wife says the stitching is coming loose already. That's defective merchandise!"

Beth picked up the garment, examining the stitching with genuine attention. "This is actually a design element—the distressed stitching is intentional in this particular style. But I completely understand if it wasn't what your wife expected."

Her fingers traced the stitching, demonstrating its intentional nature with the confidence of someone who knew her products inside and out. Mitch found himself admiring her composure—where many would have become defensive, Beth remained calm and solution-focused.

"Look, I don't want store credit. I want my money back." The man's volume increased again, causing several browsing customers to glance over nervously.

"I wish I could make an exception, but—" Beth began.

"But nothing! This is terrible customer service! I'll make sure everyone knows how you treat people!"

Beth took a deep breath. When she spoke again, her voice remained level, but there was a new firmness to it.

"Mr. Collins, I value all my customers, which is why our policies are clearly printed on every receipt. I'm trying to offer a reasonable solution. Perhaps we could look at—"

"I don't want to look at anything else in this overpriced boutique!" The man's face had gone from red to purple. He snatched the shirt from the counter and threw it down. "This is ridiculous! I want to speak to the owner!"

"I am the owner," Beth replied, quiet dignity in every syllable.

Something in the man's expression changed—a flash of surprise, then renewed determination. He leaned closer. "Well then, little lady, maybe you should learn how to run a proper business."

The patronizing tone made Mitch's jaw clench. He stepped forward, deciding it was time to intervene, but Beth's voice stopped him.

"Mr. Collins," she said, with a calm that seemed to fill the entire store, "I understand you're disappointed. That matters to me. But speaking to me disrespectfully won't change our return policy." She picked up the shirt and folded it. "I'm offering store credit as a courtesy, despite being outside our return window. That's the best I can do."

The man opened his mouth, closed it, then glared. "This isn't over," he muttered, but some of the fight had left him.

Mitch chose that moment to approach. "Is there a problem?" he asked, his tone conversational but carrying the weight of his authority.

Mr. Collins turned, registering the uniform with visible surprise. "This woman won't give me a refund."

"Ms. Rutledge has her own store policies, just like every other business does." He gestured to the shirt. "Looks like she's offered a fair alternative with store credit."

"But—"

"Sir," Mitch continued, his voice remaining even, "I understand it's frustrating when things don't go as planned. But raising your voice and making threats isn't going to improve the situation."

The man's shoulders sagged slightly. "I wasn't threatening anybody," he grumbled, though with less conviction.

"Good to hear," Mitch said. "Now, are you interested in the store credit Ms. Rutledge offered, or would you prefer to take your shirt and think about it?"

Beth watched the interaction with quiet interest, noting how Mitch never raised his voice or used his physical presence to intimidate—yet his calm authority seemed to clear the air like a summer breeze after a thunderstorm.

Mr. Collins glanced between them, then sighed heavily. "Fine. Store credit." He directed a stiff nod toward Beth. "My wife can find something else, I suppose."

"Wonderful," Beth said, professional warmth returning to her voice as she processed the transaction. "The credit is good for six months, and we get new merchandise weekly. Please tell your wife she's welcome to come in anytime."

After the man left, clutching his store credit receipt with lingering reluctance, Beth turned to Mitch. "Thank you for that," she said. "Though I think I had it under control."

"You absolutely did," Mitch agreed, surprising her. "I've seen officers with fifteen years' experience handle a confrontation with less skill."

A slight flush colored her cheeks at the unexpected praise. "I've had practice. Retail teaches you a lot about human nature—good and bad."

"So does law enforcement," Mitch said with a small smile. "I actually came by to give you some information about security options."

Beth glanced around the store. The confrontation had disrupted the peaceful shopping atmosphere, but things were settling back into normal. Pearl was straightening a display, while Alisha had smoothly returned to helping a customer choose between two scarves.

"I could use a break, honestly," Beth admitted. "That kind of interaction takes more out of me than I like to admit."

"Understandable," Mitch said. An idea formed, one that surprised him with its suddenness. "A cup of Martha's coffee might help take the edge off."

Beth's eyebrows lifted slightly.

"To discuss security measures," he clarified quickly. "Professionally speaking."

A hint of amusement touched her eyes. "Of course. Professionally speaking." She turned to Alisha. "Can you and Pearl handle things for about an hour?"

"Absolutely," Alisha replied, a curious glance flickering between Beth and Mitch. "Take your time. It's the mid-afternoon lull, anyway."

"Let me just grab my purse," Beth said.

As she disappeared down the hall heading toward her office, Pearl sidled up beside Mitch, arranging a scarf display with deliberate slowness. "That was nicely handled, Sheriff," she said, her voice pitched low. "Both the angry customer and the invitation for coffee."

"It's just coffee to discuss security options," Mitch corrected, feeling oddly defensive.

Pearl's knowing smile reminded him of his grandmother. "Mm-hmm. And I'm just arranging scarves, not eavesdropping."

Beth returned before Mitch could respond, her purse slung over her shoulder. "Ready?"

The walk to the diner was short—just three storefronts down the sidewalk—but Mitch found himself very aware of Beth's presence beside him. Her floral scent mingled with the warm summer air, and he noticed how she matched his naturally long stride without effort.

"That customer," Mitch said as they walked. "Has he caused problems before?"

Beth shook her head. "Not that I recall. Most customers are wonderful, but there's always that ten percent who think the rules don't apply to them."

"Same in my line of work," Mitch agreed. "Though the stakes are usually higher than a return policy."

"I suppose they are," Beth acknowledged. "Though that shirt probably felt like high stakes to him at the moment."

Mitch glanced at her with new appreciation. Many people would have simply labeled the man as unreasonable, but Beth's perspective showed empathy even after being treated poorly.

The diner was moderately busy with the late lunch crowd. Martha spotted them immediately, her eyebrows rising as she noted their arrival together. She gestured to a booth by the window, away from the main cluster of customers.

"Well, this is a pleasant surprise," Martha said as they settled into the booth. "Coffee for both?"

"Please," Mitch said.

"And maybe a slice of whatever pie is fresh?" Beth added with a small smile.

"Apple... just came out of the oven twenty minutes ago," Martha replied, her eyes twinkling. "Whipped cream?"

"Is there any other way?"

After Martha left to fetch their order, an awkward silence settled between them.

"So," Beth said, neatly arranging the sugar packets in their container, "these security options?"

Mitch opened the folder he had set on the table. "I've put together some information from local security companies. Different options at different price points." He slid the folder across the table. "The first one is what I'd recommend—cameras covering the main areas, particularly near the jewelry displays and register."

Beth scanned the page with careful attention. "This is... remarkably thorough."

"Just doing my job," Mitch said automatically.

Beth looked up, a curious expression crossing her face. "Is compiling security vendor information for local businesses typically part of the sheriff's duties?"

Caught, Mitch felt a flush of warmth at the back of his neck. "Not typically, no."

A small smile played at the corners of her mouth. "I see."

Martha returned with their coffee and a generous slice of apple pie topped with a cloud of whipped cream for Beth. "Here you go, dears. Anything else you need?"

"This looks perfect, Martha," Beth said. "Thank you."

When Martha had moved on to another table, Beth picked up her fork and took a small bite of pie, closing her eyes briefly in appreciation. "This almost makes dealing with difficult customers worthwhile."

Mitch watched her enjoyment, finding it oddly satisfying. "You really handled him well. Better than most would have."

"I can't control how others behave, only how I respond." Beth stirred the cream into her coffee. "Though I admit there are moments when I'm tempted to be less gracious."

"That restraint is a strength," Mitch said. "Especially in situations where emotions are high."

Beth studied him over the rim of her coffee cup. "You didn't escalate the situation, either. No threats, no intimidation. Just... presence and reason."

"Threats generally make things worse, not better." Mitch shrugged. "Besides, most people just want to be heard and respected, even when they're wrong."

"Is that what you've learned as sheriff? That most people just want respect?"

Mitch considered the question, appreciating its thoughtfulness. "That, and most people are doing the best they can with what they know at the time. Even when that 'best' looks pretty terrible from the outside."

Beth's expression softened. "That's... surprisingly compassionate."

"Don't tell anyone," Mitch said, a hint of dry humor in his voice. "I have a reputation to maintain."

Her laugh was warm and genuine, lighting up her face in a way that made something shift in Mitch's chest. "Your secret's safe with me, Sheriff."

"Mitch," he reminded her. "So, the toy store space. Have you made a decision about it?"

Beth's expression brightened. "I'm meeting with the landlord again soon. I'm still terrified, but leaning toward yes."

"What's the scariest part?" Mitch asked.

"Failing," she admitted immediately. "Overextending myself. Making another poor judgment call." She gave a self-deprecating smile. "Take your pick."

"From what I've seen of Mountain Chic, your judgment in business matters seems pretty sound."

"Business, maybe," Beth said, her voice dropping slightly. "Personal matters are another story."

Martha appeared at their table with a coffee pot, refilling their cups without asking. "You two need anything else?"

"I'm good, thank you," Beth said with a smile.

"Just the check when you get a chance," Mitch added.

"Oh, now there's no need to rush... you both sit there and enjoy your time together," Martha replied, her gaze bouncing meaningfully between them before she moved away.

Beth shook her head with a small laugh. "Martha's about as subtle as a freight train."

"She means well," Mitch said. "Though I suspect we'll be the topic of gossip for the next week."

"Just a week? You're optimistic." Beth's smile faded slightly. "Does that bother you? The potential gossip, I mean."

Mitch considered the question. "It comes with being sheriff in a small town. People talk. Mostly it's harmless."

"And when it's not harmless?"

"Then I remember that most people commenting on my life haven't walked in my shoes," Mitch said. "Their opinions matter less than doing what, I believe, is right."

Beth studied him with renewed interest. "That's a healthy perspective."

"Not always easy to maintain," he admitted. "But necessary."

"Necessary," Beth echoed, a thoughtful expression crossing her face. "You know, when you first came into my store, I thought you were..."

"Overbearing?" Mitch supplied when she hesitated.

"I was going to say overprotective," Beth corrected with a slight smile. "But I'm beginning to think I misjudged you."

"In what way?"

"I assumed your protective instincts came from the same place as..." She paused, choosing her words carefully. "As men who think women need controlling rather than supporting. But that's not you at all, is it?"

The insight surprised him with its accuracy. "Protection without control is what I aim for, both as sheriff and... in life, in general."

"It's a significant quality. One I'm learning to recognize."

Martha returned with their check, which Mitch took before Beth could reach for it.

"I invited you," he said when she began to protest. "Professional consultation."

A smile quirked her lips. "Is that what we're calling it?"

"For now," Mitch replied, surprising himself with his boldness.

Beth's cheeks colored slightly, but she didn't look away. "I should get back to the store."

"Of course." Mitch stood, leaving enough cash to cover their bill and a generous tip. "I hope the security information is helpful."

"It is," Beth said, gathering the folder as she rose. "Though I think the break for a cup of coffee with you might have been even more valuable."

They walked back to Mountain Chic in comfortable silence. At the boutique door, Beth paused.

"Thank you," she said.

"My pleasure," Mitch replied, meaning it. "If you have questions about any of those security options, please let me know."

Beth nodded and turned to enter her store.

"Pastor Andrew's new adult Bible Study starts this Friday... are you going?" Mitch asked.

"I planned on going," she said as she turned back to face him.

"Good, I'll see you there."

"Right." Beth tucked a strand of hair behind her ear. "Well, thank you again."

Chapter 7

Mitch shifted in the folding chair, the cheap metal frame creaking beneath him. Pastor Andrew's voice faded in and out of his awareness as his gaze kept drifting across the circle of chairs to where Beth sat, her blonde hair catching the warm light from the recreation hall's overhead fixtures. She was focused on the Bible in her lap, nodding occasionally at something Pastor Andrew said.

The recreation hall behind Laurel Ridge Community Church buzzed with the gentle hum of the aging air conditioning unit fighting against the July heat. About twenty people sat in a circle of folding chairs—some familiar faces from around town, others Mitch only recognized from Sunday services. His brother Cody sat beside him, thumbing through the Bible that Pastor Andrew had handed him when they arrived, looking slightly uncomfortable but making an effort.

Pastor Andrew's voice broke through Mitch's wandering thoughts.

"So what do you all think Paul meant when he wrote about putting on the full armor of God?" Pastor Andrew asked, his gaze sweeping the community members sitting in the surrounding circle. "Mitch, you've been quiet tonight. Any thoughts?"

The direct question jerked Mitch's attention back to the discussion. He cleared his throat, grateful he'd actually been semi-following along despite his distraction.

"I think it's about preparation," he said. "In law enforcement, we don't wait until there's danger to put on protective gear. We wear it knowing threats exist, even when we can't see them."

Pastor Andrew nodded encouragingly. "Good insight. Anyone else?"

"I've always thought of it as a daily choice," Beth said, her voice carrying clearly through the room. "Choosing truth over lies, and faith over fear, each morning before facing the world."

Mitch nodded in agreement. Her interpretation resonated with his own experience—the daily decision to trust God despite life's disappointments.

"Both excellent points," Pastor Andrew said. "Paul's metaphor reminds us that spiritual preparation isn't optional—it's essential. Just as Mitch wouldn't send his deputies out without proper equipment, God doesn't send us into life's battles unprepared."

The discussion continued, with Martha offering a perspective about how the "sword of the Spirit" had helped her through grief after losing her husband, and Leslie sharing how the "shield of faith" had protected her during a particularly difficult season of her life.

Mitch tried to focus, but his attention kept returning to Beth. She'd worn her hair down tonight, and it fell in soft waves past her shoulders. When she laughed at something Leslie said, it made him smile.

Cody elbowed him subtly. "You're staring," he whispered.

Mitch shifted his gaze to his Bible, pretending to find a passage. His brother's knowing smirk wasn't helping matters.

"Let's wrap up with prayer," Pastor Andrew said, bringing Mitch's wandering thoughts back to the present. "Would anyone like to lead us tonight?"

Beth raised her hand. "I will."

As the group bowed their heads, her voice filled the quiet room. "Father, thank You for Your protection that goes beyond what we can see or understand. When we face uncertainty or fear, help us remember to put on Your armor first—Your truth, Your righteousness, Your peace. Remind us that no matter what challenges we face, You've already prepared us with everything we need. Amen."

A chorus of amens followed. As people began gathering their things, the atmosphere shifted from reverent to social. The scent of coffee and fresh-baked cookies wafted from the back table near the kitchen, where church volunteers had set up refreshments.

Mitch stood, stretching slightly to relieve the stiffness from sitting too long in the uncomfortable chair. Cody rose beside him, already scanning the room.

"Those cookies smell amazing," his brother said. "I'm going to grab some before they disappear."

"Save some for the rest of us," Mitch replied, but Cody was already weaving through the dispersing circle toward the refreshment table.

Mitch watched as Beth chatted with Leslie near the window. The evening sunlight streaming through the blinds cast alternating stripes of light and shadow across their faces. Before he could talk himself out of it, he headed for the coffee station.

He poured two cups, adding cream to one. Taking a deep breath, he crossed the room to where Beth and Leslie stood.

"Coffee?" he offered, extending the creamed cup toward Beth.

Beth looked surprised, but pleased. "Thank you. That's thoughtful."

Leslie's eyebrows shot up. "Well, I think I'll go see what Martha's saying that has everyone laughing so hard." She squeezed Beth's arm before disappearing toward the refreshment table, leaving them alone.

"Your prayer was nice," Mitch said, then immediately felt foolish. *Nice? Was that the best he could do?*

Beth didn't seem to mind. "Thanks. Your comment about preparation really resonated with me. I've never thought about it from a law enforcement perspective before."

"Occupational hazard," Mitch said with a slight smile. "I tend to see most things through that lens."

"It's a useful perspective," Beth replied. "Especially with Paul's metaphor." She took a sip of her coffee. "Perfect. How did you know I take cream?"

"Sheriff's observation skills," Mitch said, the corner of his mouth lifting. "That, and I saw you add it at Martha's the other day."

"Impressive memory," Beth said, her eyes warming with something that made Mitch's pulse quicken.

"Mitch, as I live and breathe," Tessa's voice broke in as she approached them, her smile bright. "I'm glad to see you hung around after bible study... I expected you would take off as soon as it ended."

"Very funny," Mitch replied, but there was no heat in his words.

Tessa turned to Beth. "He's usually too busy protecting the town to join any social functions. I'm beginning to think there might be a special reason." Her meaningful glance between them made Beth's cheeks flush pink.

"I just felt like hanging around and chatting afterward, Tessa," Mitch said.

"Beth, the new sundress I purchased from you a few weeks is exquisite," Tessa said, smoothly changing the subject. "I've already worn it twice."

"I'm glad you like it," Beth replied. "That shade of blue was perfect for you."

"Beth has an eye for what looks good on people," Tessa told Mitch. "It's like a superpower."

"A useful one," Mitch agreed, his gaze lingering on Beth's eyes.

"Hey sis," Cody's voice boomed as he joined their small circle, a plate piled high with cookies in one hand. "Mrs. Henderson still makes the best snickerdoodles."

Tessa laughed. "Still thinking with your stomach, I see, dear brother."

"Some things are constant," Cody replied with a grin. He turned to Beth. "I don't think we've met. I'm Cody, the superior Baker sibling."

"In your dreams," Tessa muttered.

Beth smiled, extending her hand. "Beth Rutledge. I own Mountain Chic on Main Street."

Cody shook her hand. "Nice to meet you. I've been away so long, I'm still relearning who's who in Laurel Ridge."

"Twelve years in the Marines, right?" Beth asked. "I vaguely remember you from school, but we were in different grades."

"Wait, Rutledge... weren't you Beth Harrison back then? Cheerleader.... Valedictorian of your senior class?"

Beth looked surprised. "That's right. I'm impressed you, remember."

"Cody has a weird memory for details," Tessa explained. "Except when it comes to remembering to return his sister's phone calls or texts."

"I get around to it sooner or later," Cody protested.

"Days later... just when I'm about to have Mitch to send out the search and rescue team," Tessa countered.

"How are you liking being back in Laurel Ridge?" Beth asked Cody.

"It's...different," Cody said, his expression turning thoughtful. "Quieter than I'm used to. But working at the hardware store is helping me adjust. Gives me something to do with my hands while my head catches up to civilian life."

Mitch watched his brother, noting the genuine response. Cody had been deflecting questions about his adjustment since returning, offering surface-level responses that revealed nothing. This small moment of honesty felt significant.

"Adjustment takes time," Beth said with understanding. "After my divorce, I felt like I was relearning how to exist in spaces that used to feel familiar. Everything looked the same, but nothing felt the same."

Cody nodded. "That's exactly it. Everyone here knows me as the wild kid who left town, but that's not who I am anymore. Not entirely, anyway."

"People will catch up to who you are now," Beth assured him. "Just give them time to see beyond their memories."

Mitch observed the exchange with interest. Beth had just given voice to something he'd been trying to understand about his brother's struggle—and Cody had actually listened.

Leslie rejoined them, slipping an arm through Beth's. "Sorry to interrupt, but Martha's asking about the flower arrangements for Vacation Bible School. Beth, you've got that color scheme eye... you and I always work well together."

Beth nodded. "Rain check Leslie... I'm exhausted this evening. I think I'll head home." She turned to Mitch and his siblings. "It was a pleasure talking to all of you. Cody, welcome home."

"I'll walk you to your car," Mitch said, the words coming out before he'd fully thought them through.

Beth looked momentarily surprised, then nodded. "That would be nice, thank you."

Tessa and Cody exchanged a look that Mitch deliberately ignored. "I'll be right back," he told them.

As Beth said her goodbyes to Pastor Andrew and his wife, Lily, Mitch waited by the door, aware of his brother's smirk and his sister's encouraging smile. He'd never felt so thoroughly transparent in his life.

The evening air had cooled slightly as he and Beth stepped outside, though the summer humidity still hung around them. Crickets chirped from the shrubs lining the church's walkway, and fireflies blinked lazily above the grass.

"Beautiful evening," Beth commented as they walked toward the parking lot.

"One of the things I love about summers here," Mitch agreed. "Even after the hottest days, the evenings usually cool off enough to be pleasant."

They walked in silence for a few moments, their footsteps crunching on the gravel lot. When they reached Beth's pearl colored SUV, she turned to face him.

"Thank you for the coffee earlier," she said. "And the conversation. Your brother seems nice."

"He is," Mitch said. "Underneath all the bravado. He's going through a lot right now, but I think he's finding his footing a little at a time."

Beth nodded. "It takes time, finding yourself again after change."

"Beth, would you join me for breakfast at Martha's tomorrow morning?"

Beth stopped rummaging in her purse for her keys, her hand going still. When she looked up, surprise was written across her features.

"This sounds an awful lot like you're asking me on a date," she said.

Mitch met her gaze steadily. "You could say that."

Beth's hand resumed its movement, finding her keys and pressing the button to unlock her doors. "I... haven't been on a date in years," she admitted. "And honestly, I'm not sure if I'm ready."

The hesitation in her voice didn't sound like rejection, so much as genuine uncertainty. Mitch nodded, trying to hide his disappointment.

"I understand," he said, reaching past her to open her car door. "No pressure."

She smiled gratefully. "Thank you for understanding." She slid into the driver's seat.

"Drive safely," Mitch said, closing her door gently.

He turned and began walking back toward the church, his mind already analyzing where he'd misread the situation. Maybe he'd been too forward, or possibly...

"Mitch!"

He turned to find Beth with her window rolled down, engine running.

"Breakfast as friends?" she called. "I could always use another friend."

A warmth spread through his chest that had nothing to do with the July evening. "Seven at Martha's?"

Beth nodded, a small smile playing at her lips. "See you in the morning."

As she drove away, Mitch stood in the parking lot longer than necessary, watching her taillights disappear down the road. When he finally began walking back, he found Cody leaning against the recreation hall door, arms crossed, and looking far too amused.

"So," his brother said as Mitch approached. "That went well."

"Shut up," Mitch replied without heat.

"You know, for the man who taught me how to talk to girls when I was fourteen, you're surprisingly awkward at this."

"I'm not awkward," Mitch protested. "I'm... cautious."

Cody snorted. "That's one word for it." His expression softened. "She seems nice, though. Worth being cautious for."

"Yeah," he agreed. "She is."

Inside, the Bible study had mostly dispersed, with just a few people helping clean up. Tessa was stacking chairs against the wall, and she raised her eyebrows questioningly when she saw him enter the building to help.

"Well?" she prompted.

"We're having breakfast tomorrow," Mitch said. "As friends."

Tessa smiled. "That's a start."

"A start?" Mitch asked, though he knew exactly what his sister meant.

"To whatever comes next," Tessa replied, handing him a folding chair to add to the stack. "Life doesn't come with guarantees, Mitch. You know that better than most. Every so often, you just have to show up and see what happens."

Pastor Andrew approached them, collecting abandoned coffee cups. "Everything alright, Mitch? You look like you're contemplating the mysteries of the universe."

"Just the mysteries of human connection," Mitch replied.

Andrew chuckled. "An equally profound subject. The Bible study today was about protective armor, but sometimes the greater courage is removing that armor when the right moment comes."

Mitch considered the pastor's words. "Even when it leaves you vulnerable?"

"Especially then," Andrew replied. "Genuine connection requires vulnerability. Can't have one without the other."

As they finished cleaning up, Mitch found himself thinking about Beth's prayer—about daily choices and unseen protection. Maybe asking her to breakfast had been his way of choosing faith over fear, truth over lies.

The lie was that he was better off alone, safer keeping everyone at a distance. The truth was that he yearned for the kind of connection he saw in others—the quiet understanding between Martha and her late husband, the easy partnership between Pastor Andrew and Lily, and even the playful bond between siblings that he'd helped foster but somehow remained outside of at times.

Back at his truck, Cody was waiting, leaning against the passenger door.

"You think too loud," his brother commented as Mitch unlocked the vehicle.

"So I've been told," Mitch replied.

They climbed in, and Mitch started the engine. As they pulled out of the church parking lot, Cody spoke again.

"You know, when I was overseas, I used to think about coming back home. About what it would be like to live a normal life again." He stared out the window at the passing trees. "I never pictured you dating, though. Always figured you'd be married to the job forever."

"It's just breakfast," Mitch said automatically.

"Sure it is," Cody replied, unconvinced. "Just like I'm just temporarily staying with you until I figure things out."

The comparison made Mitch glance at his brother. "What's that supposed to mean?"

Cody shrugged. "Just that sometimes 'temporary' and 'just' are words we used to make big things feel smaller and less scary."

When had his younger brother gotten so insightful? Mitch wondered. The Cody who'd left Laurel Ridge at eighteen had been all impulse and action, with little reflection. The man beside him now carried the weight of experiences Mitch could only imagine.

"Maybe you're right," Mitch conceded after a moment.

"Write this date down," Cody said with a grin. "My big brother actually admitted I might be right about something."

Mitch shook his head, but smiled despite himself. "Don't get used to it."

As they drove through town, the lights of Main Street businesses glowed warmly against the deepening twilight. They passed Mountain Chic, its windows dark now that the store was closed.

Mitch thought about Beth sitting across from him tomorrow morning at Martha's. Friend or something more, the prospect of spending time with her filled him with anticipation.

When they reached the turnoff to their home, Cody broke the silence.

"For what it's worth," he said, "I think she'd be good for you."

"Why's that?" Mitch asked, genuinely curious.

Cody considered for a moment. "Because when you were talking to her tonight, you didn't look like Sheriff Baker. You just looked like Mitch. It's been a while since I've seen that guy."

The observation lingered in Mitch's mind long after they'd arrived home, even as he went through his evening routine—checking locks, letting Duke out for one last patrol of the yard, and trying to read a few chapters of the mystery novel on his nightstand.

As he finally drifted toward sleep, he found himself wondering if he could be the kind of man worthy of someone like Beth Rutledge—not just Sheriff Baker with his duty and responsibility, but Mitch, with all his flaws and hopes and carefully guarded heart.

Chapter 8

Beth stood before her full-length mirror, staring at the fourth outfit she'd tried on that morning—a sky-blue blouse paired with white capris—and promptly yanked them off. The discarded clothes formed a small mountain on her bed, a testament to her indecision.

"This is ridiculous," she muttered, glancing at the bedside clock. Six-fifteen. She'd been at this for nearly an hour. "I'm thirty-four, not sixteen."

She sat on the edge of her bed, pushing aside a rejected summer cardigan. What was she doing? It was just breakfast with a friend. A very tall, handsome new friend with kind eyes and broad shoulders who happened to wear a sheriff's badge very well.

"Just friends," she reminded herself firmly, the words echoing in her quiet bedroom.

After another moment of deliberation, she selected a simple sundress in a soft coral shade—casual enough for breakfast, but cute and comfortable. As she slipped it over her head, her phone rang. Leslie's name flashed on the screen.

"Morning, early bird," Beth answered, tucking the phone between her ear and shoulder as she smoothed the dress.

"Mornin'! I'm heading to Charleston for a flower market and wondered if you wanted to join me? We could make a day of it, maybe even do some shopping at that boutique you liked last time."

Beth hesitated. "That sounds fun, but I actually have plans."

"Oh?" Leslie's voice lifted with interest. "What kind of plans or do you mean work... that you could quite possibly take a day off from? You know Pearl and Alisha are quite capable of running the store?"

"Breakfast plans."

"Breakfast," Leslie repeated slowly. "With whom?"

Beth sighed, knowing her friend wouldn't let it go. "Sheriff Baker."

The squeal that came through the phone made Beth hold it away from her ear. "I knew it! Martha called me last night and said she had twenty dollars riding on you two going on a date before the end of the week."

"Martha has a bet—wait, who's she betting with?"

"Pearl, of course. Pearl said you wouldn't agree to a date so soon. Guess she lost the bet..."

Beth sat back down on her bed. "It's not a date. We're having breakfast as friends."

"And I bet you've been up since the crack of dawn getting ready for 'just breakfast'?"

"How did you—" Beth looked around her room suspiciously, as if Leslie might be watching through the window.

"Because I know you," Leslie laughed. "I know how you overthink things."

"I don't know if I'm ready for this," Beth admitted quietly.

"Ready or not, you're trying on clothes and having breakfast with the handsomest bachelor in town."

"It's not like that," Beth insisted, though her reflection in the mirror—cheeks flushed, eyes bright—suggested otherwise.

"It never is, until suddenly, it is," Leslie said. "Just... don't close the door before seeing what's on the other side, okay?"

After they hung up, Beth finished getting ready, applying minimal makeup and leaving her hair down in soft waves. At the last moment, she reached for the small jewelry box on her dresser and withdrew her grandmother's silver pendant—a delicate oval with a tiny pearl nestled in its center.

"A little courage couldn't hurt," she whispered, fastening it around her neck.

"Lord," she prayed softly, "grant me wisdom today. Guard my heart against foolishness, but also against fear. And please... please help me to be calm and not make a fool of myself. Amen."

The simple prayer steadied her as she gathered her purse and keys. Friendship was a safe beginning. She could do friendship.

***

Beth sat in her car, watching the minutes change on her dashboard clock. Six fifty-five.

"This is silly," she told herself, reaching for the door handle. "You've been to Martha's a thousand times."

But never like this, a small voice whispered in her mind.

The diner was quieter than usual, occupied by just a handful of early risers—Mr. Williams, with his newspaper in the corner booth, a couple of construction workers at the counter, and Dorothy Henderson arranging programs for Sunday's church service.

Martha looked up from wiping down the counter, her face breaking into a warm smile. "Well, good morning, sunshine! You're out and about early for a Saturday."

"Morning, Martha," Beth replied, suddenly self-conscious under the older woman's knowing gaze. "Could I get a booth, please?"

"Of course, honey. Eating alone today?"

Beth hesitated. "Actually, someone's meeting me."

Martha's eyebrows rose, her smile widening. "Is that so? Well, let's get you that corner booth by the window. Best view in the house." She led Beth to the table, setting down two menus. "Coffee while you wait?"

"Please," Beth nodded, sliding into the booth.

Martha returned with a steaming mug. "I have a feeling you're waiting on Mitch... he's never late, honey. He'll be here any minute, I promise," she said with a wink before bustling back to the kitchen.

Beth wrapped her hands around the warm ceramic, watching Main Street through the window as Laurel Ridge awakened. A young mother pushed a stroller past, waving to someone down the sidewalk. A couple jogged past with their dog on a leash. The familiar rhythms of her hometown unfolded like a well-loved book.

And then Mitch appeared, walking toward the diner with purposeful strides. His uniform was crisp, the sheriff's badge catching the morning light. But it was his face that held Beth's attention when he caught sight of her through the window.

Something fluttered in her chest, a quick wing-beat of anticipation that she immediately tamped down. *Friends,* she reminded herself firmly.

Martha called a greeting, and several diner patrons nodded respectfully as he made his way to Beth's booth. She noticed how people responded to him—with deference but also genuine warmth. He wasn't just respected in Laurel Ridge; he was well-liked.

"Morning," he said, sliding into the seat across from her. "Have you been waiting long?"

"Just a few minutes," Beth replied, surprised at how natural her voice sounded despite the nervous energy humming through her.

Martha appeared with another mug of coffee. "Here you go, Mitch." She set it down with a motherly pat on his shoulder. "You two know what you're having yet?"

"I think we need another minute," Beth said, reaching for her menu.

"Take your time," Martha replied, her gaze bouncing between them with undisguised interest. "The biscuits just came out of the oven. Just saying."

After she left, a momentary awkwardness settled between them. Mitch cleared his throat. "So," he began, "friends have breakfast all the time, right?"

The directness of his statement, acknowledging the slight absurdity of their situation, made Beth smile. "Absolutely. Very normal friend activity."

"Exactly what I was thinking," he agreed, his expression relaxing into something warmer.

Martha returned with her order pad. "Decided yet?"

"Biscuits and gravy," they said in unison, then exchanged surprised glances.

Martha's eyebrows shot up. "Well, look at that. Already thinking alike." She jotted down their order. "Friends, huh? Well, you both need proper feeding, regardless of what you're calling yourselves."

As Martha walked away, Beth felt a flush creeping up her neck as she watched her go. "Is it just me, or does everyone seem very invested in our breakfast?"

Mitch glanced around, noting the curious glances from the other patrons. "Small town," he said with a rueful smile. "Nothing stays private for long."

"That's both comforting and terrifying," Beth admitted.

"Mostly terrifying when you're a teenager sneaking home past curfew and your father is friends with every neighbor on the block," Mitch said, a hint of humor warming his voice.

"Is that the voice of experience talking?" Beth asked, intrigued by this glimpse into young Mitch Baker.

He nodded, relaxing back against the booth. "Dad had a sixth sense about teenage mischief. Probably why I never got away with much."

"I can't imagine you getting into trouble," Beth said. "You seem so…"

"Responsible?" he supplied. "Rule-following? Boring?"

"I was going to say 'steady,'" Beth corrected gently. "There's something reassuring about knowing exactly where you stand with someone."

"That means a lot coming from you."

The arrival of their food provided a welcome diversion from the sudden intensity between them. Martha set down two plates heaped with fluffy biscuits smothered in creamy sausage gravy, the aroma rich and savory.

"Eat up while it's hot," Martha instructed. "And holler if you need anything else."

They both dove into their breakfast, the first few bites accompanied by appreciative murmurs rather than conversation. The familiar comfort food seemed to ease the remaining tension, and soon they settled into more natural dialogue.

"So," Mitch said, "how's the security system search coming along?"

"The cameras go in on Monday," Beth replied. "Thank you again for the recommendations. The company you suggested offered me a great price on a system and even gave me a discount."

"Earl's son installed the same system at the hardware store last year. Says it's user-friendly, too."

Beth nodded. "Speaking of Earl, how's your brother really doing at the store?"

"Good," Mitch admitted, surprising Beth with his candor. "Earl told me yesterday that Cody has a knack for the mechanical aspects of the job. He's been fixing things customers bring in, not just selling products."

"That sounds perfect for someone transitioning from military service. Using existing skills while learning new ones."

Mitch studied her over his coffee mug.

Beth hesitated, considering how much to share. "After my divorce, I had to figure out which parts of my life still worked and which needed rebuilding. Using what I already knew gave me confidence to face the newness of it all."

"I'm sorry you went through that," Mitch said, his voice gentle.

Beth traced the rim of her mug with one finger. "It was... educational, I suppose. Not the learning experience I would have chosen, but..." she trailed off, still finding it difficult to discuss Matt's betrayal without emotion creeping into her voice.

"But it shaped who you are now," Mitch finished for her.

"Yes," she agreed, looking up at him. "Though sometimes I wonder if I'll ever trust my own judgment again."

Mitch's gaze held hers, steady and without pity. "Trust is rebuilt the same way it's initially formed—one small decision at a time."

The simple wisdom of his statement resonated with Beth and made her smile.

"That's one thing my father instilled in me," Mitch nodded. "He always said fear makes good servants but terrible masters."

"Smart man."

"He really was," Mitch agreed.

Dorothy Henderson chose that moment to approach their table, church programs clutched to her chest and eyes bright with curiosity.

"Good morning, you two," she greeted them. "What a lovely surprise to see you both here so early." Her gaze moved between them, missing nothing. "My, what a handsome couple you make."

Beth opened her mouth to correct the assumption, but Mitch spoke first.

"Just friends having breakfast, Mrs. Henderson," he said smoothly. "Though I appreciate the compliment all the same."

Dorothy's expression suggested she wasn't fooled. "Well, friendship is a wonderful beginning. George and I were friends for a full year before he worked up the courage to ask me to the Harvest Dance." She patted Beth's shoulder. "See you both at church tomorrow?"

"We'll be there," Beth assured her.

As Dorothy moved away, Mitch leaned forward. "Sorry about that."

"It's fine," Beth said, surprising herself with how genuinely unbothered she felt. "She means well."

"Most people around here do," Mitch agreed. "Even when they're all up in your business."

Their conversation drifted to lighter topics—Beth's love of hiking, and Mitch's hobby of restoring old furniture in his barn. She found herself genuinely laughing at his dry humor, discovering a playfulness beneath his serious exterior that few probably witnessed.

"I still can't believe you restored that bookcase in my store," Beth said, recalling the beautiful oak piece that had been a fixture in her store for years. "I bought it at the church fundraiser auction. I remember one of the volunteers saying a 'local craftsman' had donated it."

"That would be me," Mitch admitted. "Dad taught all of us woodworking. Said working with your hands clears the mind."

"It's like hiking for me—gets me out of my own head when I'm overthinking things."

"Do you overthink things often?" Mitch asked, a subtle teasing note in his voice.

"Only every waking moment," Beth admitted with a self-deprecating smile.

Their hands reached for the salt shaker simultaneously, fingers brushing. The brief contact sent an unexpected warmth up Beth's arm, and she pulled back slightly.

"Sorry," Mitch said, immediately yielding the salt to her.

"No, you go ahead," Beth insisted.

A strand of hair fell across her cheek as she shook her head. Without thinking, Mitch reached across the table and gently tucked it behind her ear, his fingertips barely grazing her skin.

The small gesture created a moment of suspended animation between them. Beth saw something shift in Mitch's expression—a questioning, a wonder, as if he too was surprised by his action.

Before either could address the moment, Earl Smith appeared beside their table, his weathered face brightening when he spotted them.

"Morning, Sheriff! Beth!" he greeted them. "Just stopped in for coffee before opening the store." He turned to Mitch. "That brother of yours is a godsend. Fixed Ms. Talbot's vacuum cleaner yesterday when everyone else said it was beyond repair."

"Glad to hear it," Mitch said, visibly grateful for the interruption. "He's always been good with mechanical things."

"The Boy's got talent," Earl agreed. "Anyway, don't let me interrupt your breakfast. Just wanted to say hello."

After Earl moved on, Pastor Andrew entered the diner, heading straight for the counter, where Martha was pouring him a to-go cup of coffee. He spotted them and walked over, his warm smile encompassing them both.

"Beautiful morning, isn't it?" he said. "Good to see you both."

"Coffee to fuel a bit of sermon writing?" Mitch asked.

Andrew nodded. "I'm in the final push. 'Finding courage to begin again when life takes unexpected turns.'"

Beth felt the pastor's words resonate with particular meaning this morning. "Sounds like one we could all use."

"The best messages are the ones we preach to ourselves first," Andrew replied with a smile. "See you both tomorrow."

As he left, Beth found herself reflecting on the pastor's words. Beginning again. Wasn't that what she was doing right now, in this booth, with this man? Testing waters she'd convinced herself were permanently closed to her?

The squawk of Mitch's radio interrupted her thoughts. He lifted it from his belt, listening to the dispatcher's voice reporting an accident on Route 16.

"Copy that," he responded. "On my way."

Beth saw the conflict play across his face—duty calling while he clearly wished to stay. "Go," she said gently. "People need you."

Gratitude filled his expression. "I'm sorry to cut this short."

"Don't be," Beth assured him. "This is part of being..." She hesitated. "Friends with the sheriff."

Mitch stood, reaching for his wallet. "I'll take care of the check—"

"No need, Sheriff," Martha called from behind the counter. "I've got your card on file. I'll run it for both."

He nodded his thanks to Martha, then turned back to Beth. "I really enjoyed this."

"Me too," she said truthfully.

"See you at church tomorrow?" The question held more than a simple inquiry about her attendance.

"I'll be there," Beth confirmed, meeting his gaze.

Mitch's hand briefly touched hers on the table—a light pressure, gone almost before she registered it. "Be safe," she found herself saying.

"Always am," he replied with a small smile before heading for the door.

Beth watched through the window as he climbed into his patrol truck and pulled away, lights flashing. The emptiness across the table felt more significant than it should for "just friends."

Martha slid into the booth opposite her, coffeepot in hand, as she refilled Beth's mug. "Well, honey?"

"Well, what?" Beth asked, though she knew exactly what Martha was asking.

"Don't play coy with me. I've known you since you were knee high to a grasshopper. Him too." Martha set the coffeepot on the table. "That man has carried everyone else's burdens since he was barely grown. Never seen him look at anyone the way he looks at you."

Beth felt her cheeks warm. "We're just—"

"Friends. So I heard," Martha interrupted. "You know, my Harold and I started as 'just friends' too. Sometimes friendship is the best foundation."

"It's complicated, Martha."

"Life always is, honey. But some complications are worth figuring out." Martha patted her hand. "Take your time. He's not going any-where."

After Martha left to tend to other customers, Beth lingered over her coffee, watching Laurel Ridge come fully awake through the window. When she paid her bill (insisting on covering her own despite Martha's protests that "Mitch would have a fit"), she stepped out into the bright morning.

Instead of heading directly to Mountain Chic, Beth turned in the opposite direction, taking a meandering path around the block. She needed a few minutes to process the breakfast, the conversations, and the gentle touches that seemed to carry more meaning than words.

Laurel Ridge looked different somehow this morning—more vi-brant and more full of possibility. She passed the old toy store, peering through the windows at the empty space that might soon be Moun-tain Chic Kids. The thought filled her with both excitement and trepidation.

New beginnings were always frightening, whether in business or in relationships. But fear had governed too many of her choices since Matt's betrayal.

A young family walked past—mother, father, and a little girl be-tween them, each holding one of her hands and swinging her playfully between steps. The child's laughter rang out, clear and joyful, in the morning air.

Beth allowed herself, just for a moment, to imagine possibilities she'd long since dismissed. Not specifically with Mitch—it was far too soon for that—but the idea that her heart might not be permanently closed to connection, to trust, and to something beyond friendship.

Her phone buzzed with a text message: Everyone's okay. Just a fender bender. Thanks for understanding.

Beth smiled as she typed her reply: How did you get my cell number? And no worries, friends understand.

She hesitated, then added: Breakfast was nice. We should do it again sometime.

His response came quickly: You gave me your cell number on the police report. I just happened to save my friend's number in my contact list. Next Saturday? Same time?

It's a date, she typed, then immediately deleted it. Sounds perfect, she sent instead.

As she tucked her phone away and continued walking around the block, Beth realized things were changing, not dramatically, not completely, but noticeably. Like the first green shoot breaking through soil after winter, tentative but determined.

Perhaps "friends" wasn't a limitation after all. Perhaps it was simply the beginning of a path she hadn't expected to walk again—a path that might lead somewhere worth the risk.

Her grandmother's pendant felt warm against her skin, a reminder of the older woman's favorite saying: *Courage isn't the absence of fear, Beth. It's moving forward despite it.*

Chapter 9

Beth navigated her way up the church steps, narrowly avoiding a collision with eight-year-old Tommy Jenkins, who raced past her in pursuit of his little sister. The white clapboard building of Laurel Ridge Community Church gleamed in the morning sunlight, its steeple reaching toward an impossibly blue July sky. She paused at the entrance, smoothing the skirt of her floral dress—the third one she'd tried on that morning.

Pastor Andrew and his wife Lily stood just inside the doorway, greeting parishioners with warm smiles. Beth had always appreciated their genuine approach to ministry—never pretentious, always accessible.

"Good morning, Beth," Pastor Andrew said, clasping her hand in both of his. "Beautiful day the Lord has made, isn't it?"

"It certainly is," Beth agreed, returning his smile.

Lily gave her a quick hug. "That color is gorgeous on you. You're absolutely glowing this morning."

Beth felt her cheeks warm. "Thank you. New dress."

With a smile, Beth moved into the sanctuary, its familiar wooden pews already filling with Laurel Ridge residents. Sunlight filtered through the stained-glass windows, casting rainbow patches across the worn wooden floor. The scent of lemon polish mingled with the fragrance of Leslie's flower arrangements adorning the altar.

Her gaze swept across the pews in a habitual scan of familiar faces. Martha sat near the front, wearing her Sunday best navy dress with a string of pearls. The Williams family occupied their usual spot on the left side, three generations filling two entire pews. Dorothy Henderson sat in the front pew on the left, arranging her Bible, notebook, and three different colored pens on her lap, ready to take meticulous notes.

Beth continued her survey until she saw a particular tall figure sitting about halfway down on the right side. Mitch wore a crisp blue dress shirt that emphasized his broad shoulders, his dark hair neatly combed. As if sensing her gaze, he looked up, a warm smile spreading across his face when he spotted her. He nodded slightly and gestured to the space beside him in the pew he shared with Tessa and Cody.

Her heart gave a little jump that she immediately tried to dismiss. Just friends, she reminded herself firmly. Still, there was something undeniably pleasant about being singled out, about being wanted in someone's company.

She made her way down the aisle, nodding greetings to neighbors and customers as she passed. When she reached the Bakers' pew, Tessa beamed at her.

"Morning, Beth!" Tessa's friendly welcome carried genuine enthusiasm.

Cody gave her a casual nod. "Morning."

Mitch shifted slightly to make room for her. "Morning, Beth."

"Good morning, everyone," Beth replied, settling into the space beside Mitch. The pew was warm where his leg had been, and she was acutely aware of his proximity as she arranged her purse and Bible. "Well, isn't this nice? Friends all sitting together for Sunday service."

She delivered the line with a hint of teasing, acknowledging their "just friends" agreement.

A slight smile played on Mitch's lips. "Exactly. Good to have a friend join us."

Something in the way he emphasized "friend" made Beth wonder if he found their arrangement as amusingly inadequate as she suddenly did. Before she could dwell on it, the organist began the prelude, signaling the start of the service.

The familiar rhythm of worship wrapped around Beth like a comfortable sweater. She found herself relaxing, her voice joining the congregation in prayer and song.

During the announcements, Pastor Andrew's enthusiasm bubbled over as he discussed the upcoming Vacation Bible School.

"This year's theme is 'Courageous Trekkers: Following God's Path,'" he explained, gesturing to the colorful banner hanging beside the pulpit. "It's going to be a wonderful journey of discovering God's guidance through life's adventures."

He continued, thanking various volunteers for their contributions before adding, "And a special thanks to Beth Rutledge for heading up our refreshment team for the Friday Fun Day, and Sheriff Mitch Baker for organizing the outdoor games! It's going to be a fantastic way to celebrate a week of learning and adventure."

Beth's head snapped up in surprise. She hadn't volunteered for this. Her questioning glance found Leslie in the choir loft, who gave her an innocent smile that confirmed exactly who had volunteered her services.

She turned to look at Mitch, who met her gaze with a slightly raised eyebrow and the smallest hint of a smile—a silent acknowledgment of their shared predicament. Rather than feeling trapped or annoyed, Beth felt an unexpected thrill at the prospect of working with him on the VBS project.

As Pastor Andrew moved into his sermon, Beth found herself deeply engaged. His message on finding courage to begin again when life takes unexpected turns resonated with her current journey—not just her potential business expansion, but also the unexpected warmth she'd been feeling toward the man beside her.

While Pastor Andrew spoke about the courage of Abraham leaving his homeland, Beth's attention occasionally drifted to Mitch. His Bible lay open on his lap, and she couldn't help noticing how well-worn the pages were. Various passages were highlighted in different colors, with small, neat notes filling the margins. This wasn't a Bible for show; it was clearly read, studied, and lived with.

She watched as he jotted down notes in a small notebook, his handwriting surprisingly neat for such large hands. There was something deeply attractive about this glimpse into his faith—not showy or performative, but genuine and personal.

When the congregation rose for a hymn, Beth opened her hymnal to "Great Is Thy Faithfulness," a song she'd known since childhood. As the first notes filled the sanctuary, she began to sing—and then nearly lost her place when she heard the voice beside her.

Mitch's deep baritone carried the melody with surprising richness and clarity. His voice wasn't overpowering, but it was confident and true, adding depth to the congregational singing.

When the hymn ended, she couldn't help leaning slightly toward him. "You have a beautiful voice."

A flush crept up his neck, and he offered a self-deprecating smile. "Thanks. I used to sing in the choir a long time ago."

This new revelation—Mitch Baker, choir member—added another layer to the complex man beside her. Each discovery felt like turning a page in a book she increasingly wanted to read cover to cover.

The remainder of the service passed in a pleasant haze, Beth's awareness of Mitch's presence beside her never quite fading. Their shoulders nearly touched when they bowed their heads for the closing prayer, and the subtle scent of his cologne—something clean and woodsy—mingled with the church's familiar smells.

As the final benediction concluded and people began to rise, shuffling hymnals and gathering belongings, Mitch turned to her.

"So, what are your plans for the rest of this fine Sunday?" he asked, his tone casual.

"My usual," Beth replied, tucking her Bible into her purse. "Pack a picnic lunch, then head out for a hike and enjoy my afternoon reading near the waterfall. Try to clear my head before the workweek hits."

It was her Sunday ritual, a practice she'd established after her divorce—time alone in nature to reset and prepare for the week ahead.

Tessa, who had been chatting with someone in the pew behind them, suddenly leaned forward. "A hike sounds lovely, Beth! Or, if you're not set on it, you could always come back to our place. We're just having a lazy Sunday." Her eyes sparkled with genuine warmth. "I always make way too much sun tea, the chicken salad is ready for sandwiches, and there are usually some leftover cookies from Cody's raids." She playfully nudged her younger brother, who rolled his eyes good-naturedly.

"It's not my fault you make them so good," Cody protested.

Mitch nodded in agreement with Tessa's invitation. "You should join us. It's nothing fancy, but the porch swing is comfortable, and my dog Duke always appreciates an extra pair of hands for fetch." His mouth quirked in a half-smile. "Besides, Cody will probably try to rope us into some yard game, and I could use an ally."

Beth hesitated, weighing her options. Her usual solitary Sunday versus an afternoon with the Baker siblings. A year ago, she would have instantly declined, retreating to safety. But something had shifted inside her, like a small tunnel with a light at the end of it, a readiness to step beyond the careful boundaries she'd drawn around her life.

"A casual Sunday afternoon at the Baker family farmhouse. Just relaxing with friends?" She let a playful smile touch her lips. "That does sound tempting." She paused, a flicker of uncertainty returning. "Are you sure I wouldn't be intruding?"

"Absolutely not!" Tessa insisted. "The more, the merrier."

"Friends..." Mitch said. His eyes held hers, warm and genuine, a shared understanding passing between them of what that word both concealed and revealed.

"Well then," Beth decided, surprising herself with how easily the words came, "I'd love to join you."

"Perfect!" Tessa clapped her hands together.

As they made their way out of the sanctuary, Beth found herself swept into the Baker family orbit with surprising ease. Cody walked ahead of them, stopping to exchange words with Earl about the hardware store's Monday delivery schedule. Tessa linked arms with her as they descended the church steps, chatting about the upcoming school year. Mitch walked beside them, occasionally acknowledging greetings from the townspeople, but mostly listening to his sister's animated words with fond amusement.

In the church parking lot, they paused beside Beth's SUV.

"Just follow us," Mitch said. "It's about twenty minutes outside town, off Baker Road."

"I'll be right behind you," Beth said, unlocking her car.

As she slid behind the wheel, watching the Bakers climb into Mitch's blue pickup truck, Beth felt a flutter of anticipation in her stomach. This was new territory—not just the visit to Mitch's home, but the ease with which she'd accepted the invitation, and the natural way she'd been included in their family circle.

Chapter 10

The drive to the Baker family farmhouse took them through Laurel Ridge's outskirts and into the surrounding countryside. Main Street's tidy storefronts gave way to residential neighborhoods, which gradually thinned until they were driving past fields and forests. Baker Road turned out to be a winding country lane that curved gently upward into the foothills of the mountains that surrounded the valley.

Beth followed Mitch's truck as it turned onto a gravel driveway marked by a simple wooden sign reading "Baker" with the house number beneath it. The driveway curved through a stand of mature oak trees before opening onto a clearing where a two-story white farmhouse stood, its wraparound porch and green shutters giving it a timeless appeal.

A large German Shepherd came bounding across the yard as the vehicles approached, tail wagging enthusiastically. Beth parked behind Mitch's truck and stepped out, immediately enveloped by the peaceful atmosphere of the property. The air smelled of fresh-cut grass and wild honeysuckle that grew along the edge of the woods. Birds called from the nearby trees, and somewhere in the distance, a woodpecker tapped rhythmically.

"This is Duke," Mitch said as he approached, nodding toward the dog who now danced around his legs. "He's friendly, and just a bit enthusiastic."

Beth extending her hand for Duke to sniff. "Hello, Duke... aren't you a handsome boy." After a brief sniff, he pushed his head against her hand, requesting pets. Beth obliged, scratching behind his ears.

"He likes you," Mitch observed.

"I've always loved animals," Beth replied. "Much less complicated than people."

"Ain't that the truth," Cody agreed, coming to join them. "Tessa's inside getting the food ready. She sent me to say make yourselves comfortable on the porch, and she'll bring everything out."

"I should go help her," Beth said, straightening up from petting Duke.

Mitch shook his head. "Try if you want, but she'll probably shoo you right back out. Tessa doesn't like anyone in her kitchen when she's putting something together."

"It's true," Cody confirmed. "Control freak tendencies run in the family." He shot his brother a pointed look.

"Speak for yourself," Mitch replied, but there was no heat in the exchange, just the comfortable banter of siblings who knew each other well.

Beth followed them onto the porch, taking in the weathered wooden floorboards, the line of rocking chairs, and the porch swing at the far end. The view from the elevation was spectacular—rolling hills stretching toward the mountains, and the silver ribbon of a creek visible in the distance.

"This is beautiful," she said, genuine appreciation in her voice. "How many acres do you have?"

"Five now," Mitch replied, leading her toward the swing. "Used to be twenty when my grandfather ran the place as a working farm. Dad sold off some of the land after Grandpa died, kept the house and the surrounding woods."

The porch swing creaked slightly as they sat down, its chains well-oiled but still bearing the gentle sounds of age and use. Duke settled at their feet with a contented sigh.

"So, this is where you grew up?" Beth asked, genuinely curious about Mitch's background.

He nodded, his gaze moving over the property with clear affection. "Born and raised. I've lived here my whole life, except when I left briefly for college after Tessa and Cody had both graduated from high school."

Beth remembered the fragments of his story she'd gathered over the years.

Cody, who had taken one of the rocking chairs, snorted. "What he means is, he put his entire life on hold to become a parent, provider, and protector for two kids who weren't always grateful for it."

"You were kids," Mitch said, the words carrying the weight of an old, familiar argument. "You weren't supposed to be grateful. You were supposed to be safe and cared for."

The simple statement revealed volumes about Mitch's character, about the sense of duty and protection that seemed woven into the very fiber of his being. Beth studied his profile, noting the quiet strength in his expression, the way his shoulders carried responsibilities both chosen and inherited.

"Well, I'm grateful now," Cody said, his tone softening. "Even if you are an overbearing control freak sometimes."

Mitch's mouth quirked in a half-smile. "Keeps you in line."

"In your dreams," Cody retorted.

The screen door opened, and Tessa emerged carrying a tray loaded with food, plates, napkins, and glasses of amber tea garnished with lemon slices. "Stop bickering and make yourselves useful," she instructed, nodding toward the tray.

Cody jumped up to help, and soon they were all settled with plates of chicken salad sandwiches, fresh fruit, and homemade potato chips. The food was simple but delicious, and the conversation flowed easily—Tessa sharing stories about kindergarten students she'd had in the past, Cody describing a complicated repair he'd figured out at the hardware store, and Mitch occasionally adding observations that made everyone laugh.

Beth felt herself relaxing into their family dynamic, charmed by the easy affection between the siblings despite their occasional teasing. It was so different from her own upbringing as an only child, and worlds away from the strained conversations that had characterized the final months of her marriage to Matt.

"So, Beth," Tessa said during a lull in the conversation, "Mitch tells us you're thinking about opening a second store?"

Beth nodded, surprised that Mitch had mentioned it. "I'm considering it. The old toy store space on Cedar Street is available, and I've been thinking about branching into children's clothing."

"That would be wonderful," Tessa enthused. "We need a store like that in town."

"That's what keeps pushing me toward doing it... there is definitely a need." Beth admitted. "But it's a big step. More overhead, more inventory to manage, employees to hire..."

"But also more opportunity," Mitch pointed out. "More families coming through your doors, more revenue streams."

"Who knew my big brother had a head for business?" Cody teased.

"I think he has a point," Beth said, looking at Mitch with fresh appreciation. "It's easy to focus on the risks and forget about the potential rewards."

"Risks are sometimes worth taking," Mitch said, meeting her gaze.

His expression made Beth wonder if they were still talking about business expansion. The air surrounding Beth grew warmer and more charged until Cody broke the moment.

"Speaking of risks," he announced, standing up, "who's up for a game of horseshoes? I've been practicing, and I think I can finally beat the Sheriff."

"You wish," Mitch replied, the competitive gleam in his eye unmistakable.

"I'm game," Tessa said, gathering empty plates. "Beth, want to join? Fair warning—these two get ridiculously competitive."

"I'd love to," Beth said, "though I should warn you, I haven't played horseshoes since high school."

"Perfect," Cody grinned. "Fresh meat. Tessa, you team up with Beth. Mitch and I will play against you."

"Oh, I see how it is," Tessa protested. "You two against us? That hardly seems fair."

"Scared?" Cody taunted.

"You wish," Tessa replied, mimicking Mitch's earlier response. "Beth and I are going to wipe the grass with you boys."

They moved to a cleared area at the side of the house where two metal stakes were set in the ground about forty feet apart. Cody retrieved a set of horseshoes from a small shed nearby.

"Ladies first," Mitch said, gesturing for Beth and Tessa to start.

"Such gentlemen," Tessa said dryly, taking a horseshoe. "Watch and learn, Beth. The key is all in the wrist."

She sent the horseshoe spinning through the air in a perfect arc. It clanged against the stake, wrapping around it for a ringer.

"Yes!" Tessa pumped her fist in celebration. "That's how it's done!"

Beth took her turn next, concentrating as she lined up her shot. The horseshoe felt heavier than she remembered, and her first throw fell short of the stake.

"Not bad," Mitch encouraged. "Try releasing a little earlier on the next one."

Cody's first throw landed close to the stake but didn't circle it. Mitch's shot, however, was precise, resulting in another ringer.

"Of course," Tessa groaned. "Mr. Perfect. Beth, don't let him intimidate you. He's been playing this game since he could walk."

The horseshoe match continued, friendly trash talk flying as freely as the horseshoes. Beth's technique improved with each round, and by the end, she was holding her own.

The final score came down to the last throw, with the women's team just two points behind. Beth lined up her shot, concentrating on the advice Mitch had given her about the release point.

"No pressure," Cody called. "Just the entire game riding on this one throw."

"Ignore him," Tessa advised. "You've got this, Beth."

Beth took a deep breath, focused on the stake, and let the horseshoe fly. It sailed through the air in a perfect arc, landing with a satisfying clang as it wrapped around the stake for a three-point ringer.

"Yes!" Tessa shrieked, grabbing Beth in a victory hug. "I knew you could do it!"

"Beginner's luck," Cody grumbled good-naturedly.

"Or maybe she's just a natural," Mitch suggested, his smile warming Beth from across the yard.

They returned to the porch, where Tessa served homemade chocolate chip cookies and more tea. Beth sat on the porch swing again, this time with Mitch beside her, their conversation drifting comfortably from topic to topic.

"So," Mitch said eventually, "are you looking forward to our Vacation Bible School assignment? Refreshments and games on Friday?"

Beth laughed. "I'm still trying to figure out how I got volunteered for that."

"Leslie," everyone said in unison, then laughed at their synchronicity.

"I don't mind, though," Beth admitted. "I love working with the kids, and Pastor Andrew puts on a great program."

"I still don't know exactly what I've signed up for. Pastor Andrew asked if I would help a couple of weeks ago. I agreed and told him to sign me up for whatever," Mitch confessed. "But I trust you'll help me figure it out."

"Partners in VBS crime," Beth agreed. "I think we could come up with some fun games that tie into the 'Courageous Trekkers' theme. Maybe an obstacle course or a treasure hunt."

"I've got some old camping equipment in the barn we could use," Mitch suggested. "Set up a tent, maybe create a nature identification station."

As they brainstormed ideas, Beth was struck by how easily they collaborated, and how their different perspectives complemented each other. Mitch had a practical approach that balanced her creative flair, and his thoughtful suggestions enhanced her initial concepts.

The afternoon stretched into early evening; the shadows lengthening across the yard. The quality of light changed, taking on the golden hue that photographers call "magic hour." Beth realized with surprise that she'd been at the Baker farm for hours, and yet she felt no urgency to leave.

Tessa and Cody had moved inside, leaving her and Mitch alone on the porch. Duke lay at their feet, occasionally lifting his head when a bird or squirrel caught his attention. The porch swing moved in a gentle rhythm, pushed occasionally by Mitch's foot against the floor-boards.

"This has been a lovely afternoon," Beth said, breaking a comfortable silence. "Thank you for including me."

"I'm glad you came."

"You have a wonderful family, Mitch. You should be proud of what you built here."

He looked slightly surprised by her comment. "Built?"

"Yes, built," she affirmed. "You kept this family together when it could have fallen apart. That's no small thing."

Mitch glanced away, clearly uncomfortable with the praise. "I just did what anyone would do."

"No," Beth said gently. "Not everyone would have sacrificed their hopes and dreams at the age of eighteen to raise two teenagers. Not anyone would have created this home where they both clearly feel safe and loved, even as adults. That's something special, Mitch. Something you should be proud of."

The sincerity in her voice seemed to reach him, and when he looked back at her, there was a vulnerability in his expression she hadn't seen before.

"That means a lot."

Beth became acutely aware of their proximity on the swing, of the warmth of his arm just inches from hers.

The porch door opened, breaking the moment as Tessa stepped out. "Beth, are you staying for dinner? I was about to start the grill."

Beth glanced at her watch, surprised at how late it had grown. "Oh, I should probably head home."

"Next time, then," Tessa said, her tone making it clear she expected there would be a next time.

"I'd like that," Beth replied, standing from the swing. "Thank you for a wonderful afternoon."

Mitch walked her to her car, Duke trotting alongside them. The evening air had cooled slightly, carrying the sweet scent of wild roses that grew along the edge of the driveway.

"I'm glad you came today," Mitch said as they reached her SUV.

"Me too," Beth replied. "It was exactly what I needed, even though I didn't know it."

They stood facing each other in the gathering twilight, neither quite ready to say goodbye. In the distance, a whippoorwill began its evening call, the plaintive notes floating through the air.

"About Friday," Mitch said. "For VBS. Maybe we should get together sometime this week to plan? I'd hate to disappoint all those kids. Pastor Andrew said there're all kinds of outdoor games and equipment in the church's storage building I can use."

"That's a good idea," Beth agreed. "Maybe, Tuesday evening? After the store closes?"

"Perfect. Martha's? Around six and we could talk over dinner?"

"Sounds good," Beth said, trying to ignore the little thrill that ran through her at the prospect.

She opened her car door, but before getting in, she turned back to him. "Mitch?"

"Yes?"

"Today was... nice. With friends."

The emphasis she placed on the final word held a touch of the same playfulness he'd used that morning in church. His smile in response was warm and knowing.

"Very nice," he agreed. "See you Tuesday, Beth."

As she drove down the winding driveway, Beth glanced in her rearview mirror. Mitch stood watching her leave, Duke at his side, both silhouetted against the backdrop of the farmhouse.

Friends, she thought again, but the word felt less like a boundary now and more like a beginning. A safe harbor from which to explore waters that seemed increasingly inviting, despite—or perhaps because of—their unknown depths.

Chapter 11

Mitch tapped his pen against the small notepad he'd set on the table, his eyes drifting toward the diner entrance for the third time in as many minutes. The familiar sounds of dishes clinking and muted conversations surrounded him, but he barely registered it. The dinner crowd had thinned slightly, leaving a pleasant hum rather than the usual rush hour cacophony.

He glanced down at his watch. 5:56 PM.

Mitch's mind wandered back to Sunday afternoon—Beth laughing as she landed the winning horseshoe, her easy conversations with Tessa, the way Duke had instantly taken to her, resting his head on her foot as they sat on the porch swing. The memory of her silhouetted against the sunset as she'd driven away lingered.

The sensation building in his chest wasn't entirely unfamiliar, but it had been dormant for so long that recognizing it felt like discovering an old possession he'd forgotten he owned. Anticipation, he realized. Simple, pleasant anticipation of seeing someone whose company he genuinely enjoyed.

"You keep looking at that door like it might disappear," Martha commented, materializing beside his booth with a fresh pot of coffee. She topped off his mug without asking. "Beth will be here, Sheriff. Don't you worry yourself."

"I'm not worried," Mitch replied, straightening the notepad that needed no straightening. "We're just meeting to plan for the final day of VBS."

Martha's knowing smile crinkled the corners of her eyes. "Of course you are. Just planning. Nothing to be nervous about at all."

"I'm not nervous," he protested, though he'd unconsciously smoothed his blue button-down shirt twice in the last five minutes.

Martha patted his shoulder. "Bless your heart, Mitch... but you are nervous, and it's rather cute, if I might say." She winked before bustling off to refill other customers' cups.

Mitch sighed, taking a sip of his coffee. Was he that transparent? Or did Martha simply know him too well after mothering him for years?

The bell above the door jingled, and Mitch looked up to see Beth enter, a small leather-bound planner clutched to her chest. She scanned the diner; her face brightening when she spotted him. She wore a simple emerald green top that brought out the green flecks in her hazel eyes, paired with white capris. Her blonde hair was pulled back in a loose ponytail, a few strands framing her face.

Mitch stood as she approached.

"Sorry if I kept you waiting," Beth said, slightly breathless as she slid into the booth across from him. "The end-of-day rush at the boutique was crazy, and we closed later than normal."

"Not at all," Mitch assured her, settling back into his seat. "Glad you could make it." He meant it more than the simple phrase conveyed.

"Well, look who it is!" Martha appeared, order pad in hand and an exaggerated look of surprise on her face. "Table for two... for planning, of course." She punctuated the word with an obvious wink. "Coffee, Beth honey? Dinner maybe?"

Beth laughed, the sound warm and genuine. "Dinner sounds wonderful, Martha. I'm starving."

"Me too," Mitch agreed. "I'll have the meatloaf special."

"Make that two," Beth added. "Your meatloaf is legendary, Martha."

"Coming right up," Martha scribbled on her pad. "You two just settle in and... plan." She emphasized the word again with unmistakable meaning before heading toward the kitchen.

"Martha is a bit more determined than usual, now isn't she?" Beth asked with a small smile.

"She's been like this since we had breakfast together. She's definitely Laurel Ridge's couple coordinator."

"Alongside Dorothy Henderson and half the church women's group," Beth added with a laugh. "Small-town life at its finest."

"True enough," Mitch agreed, then tapped his notepad. "So, VBS. 'Courageous Trekkers.' I was thinking about that obstacle course idea from Sunday." He turned the pad so she could see the rough sketch he'd made of stations and the list of potential supplies. "Pastor Andrew showed me what's in the church storage—there are ropes we could use for a 'spider web' crossing, old tires, and I've got a pop-up tent we could set up as a 'cave' of sorts."

Beth leaned forward, her interest visibly piqued. "I love that! What if we add a 'river crossing'? We could use a blue tarp with stepping stones—maybe those flat rubber discs from the church gym?"

"Perfect," Mitch said, jotting down her suggestion. "And maybe a small 'mountain climb' with those portable steps from the recreation hall."

"Yes!" Beth's enthusiasm was contagious. "And we could tie Bible verses about courage to each station. 'Be strong and courageous' at the mountain climb, 'When you pass through the waters' at the river crossing..."

Their hands brushed as they both reached to point at different areas of the sketch. Beth didn't pull away immediately, and neither did Mitch. The brief contact sent a pleasant warmth up his arm.

"Oh!" Beth sat up straighter, eyes bright with inspiration. "We could have a 'Feed the Lions' beanbag toss for Daniel in the lion's den!"

Mitch grinned. "As long as I don't have to dress up like a lion."

"Now there's an image for VBS!" Beth laughed, her eyes crinkling at the corners. "Sheriff Baker in a lion costume. The kids would never forget it."

"And neither would Deputy Dunbar, who would make sure photos circulated through the entire department," Mitch added dryly.

Their laughter mingled naturally as they continued brainstorming, adding ideas to the growing list. Mitch found himself enjoying the collaborative energy between them, the way Beth built on his suggestions and offered creative angles he wouldn't have considered.

Martha arrived with their meals, setting steaming plates of meatloaf, mashed potatoes, and green beans before them. "You two look like you're having fun," she observed. "VBS planning must be more enjoyable than I remember."

"It is with the right planning partner," Beth replied, her gaze meeting Mitch's briefly before she turned her attention to her food.

As they began eating, Mitch decided to shift to more personal territory. "Tessa and Cody truly enjoyed having you over on Sunday. Tessa's already planning what to make next time you come for a 'friends' afternoon." He emphasized the word slightly, watching for her reaction.

A hint of pink colored Beth's cheeks, but her smile was genuine. "I had a wonderful time. Your place is so peaceful. And Duke is just the best." She took a bite of meatloaf before continuing. "Tessa has such a warm way about her. I can see why kindergartners that have her as a teacher adore her."

"She's always been the heart of our family," Mitch acknowledged. "Even when we were kids, she was the peacemaker, especially between Cody and me."

"Did you two fight a lot growing up?"

"Not fight so much as... clash," Mitch corrected. "After Mom left, I had to be both brother and parent. Cody resented the parent part, especially."

Beth nodded in understanding. "That couldn't have been easy for either of you. But look at you now—you seem to have a deep bond. You did something right."

Her observation warmed him. Few people recognized the complexity of his relationship with his siblings—most just saw the Sheriff and his family, not the years of struggle and growth it had taken to reach their current equilibrium.

"How was your day at the boutique?" he asked, redirecting the conversation to her world.

"The new system is working perfectly," Beth replied, brightening at the mention of her store. "The installation team was so professional—thank you again for the recommendation. And today we had a really good day for sales, which is unusual for a Tuesday. A tour bus from Beckley stopped around four this evening, and suddenly, we had twenty women and their spouses all shopping at once."

"Hence the late closing," Mitch observed.

They continued eating, conversation flowing naturally between VBS planning and personal topics. Mitch found himself leaning forward slightly, drawn in by Beth's animated descriptions and thoughtful insights.

"So, for the refreshments," Beth said, consulting her planner, "Leslie said the church is providing water and lemonade. They also have trail mix for Friday, and I think some cookies would be good. Maybe some fruit skewers too?"

"Sounds good," Mitch agreed. "The church has a bunch of coolers and tables. Pastor Andrew asked me to pick up ice on Friday. You focus on the 'courageous' snacks. I'll handle setting up the tables and make sure the coolers are cleaned and ready for use."

Beth laughed at his phrasing. "Courageous snacks? Is that what we're calling them?"

"Well, they have to fit the theme, right?" Mitch grinned. "Brave bananas, daring donuts..."

"Fearless fruit skewers," Beth added, playing along.

"You're getting the hang of it."

Their shared laughter drew glances from a nearby tables.

"I can bring over the camping gear from my barn on Thursday evening if you want to see if it'll work for the 'base camp' station," Mitch offered.

"That would be great," Beth agreed. "I can meet you at the church, then?"

"Perfect. Say around six?"

"I'll be there."

Mitch found himself simply watching Beth as she talked about her ideas for decorating the refreshment table with explorer-themed items. The enthusiasm that lit her features, the thoughtful way she considered each detail—it was captivating. He'd always known Beth was attractive, but seeing her passion and creativity in action revealed layers of beauty beyond the physical.

"What?" Beth asked, catching his gaze.

"Nothing," Mitch said, slightly embarrassed at being caught staring. "Just... impressed by you. The kids are going to love this VBS finale."

It struck Mitch how comfortable he felt in Beth's presence. She made him feel as if he were the only person in the world. Her genuine warmth and vibrant energy radiated across the table.

As they finished their meals, Martha approached. "Room for my apple crumble? Just came out of the oven."

Beth looked at Mitch. "Share one? I'm full but can't resist Martha's apple crumble."

"Deal," Mitch agreed.

Martha's eyebrows shot up. "Sharing dessert already? My, my, how things progress..." She shuffled off before either could respond.

"She's incorrigible," Beth said with a shake of her head.

"Always has been," Mitch agreed. "Even when I was a teenager, she was trying to match me up with every eligible girl in town."

"And did she succeed?" Beth asked, curiosity evident in her tone.

"Once or twice," Mitch admitted. "Though none of them stuck."

"Their loss," Beth said quietly.

The apple crumble arrived before Mitch could respond, steam rising from the golden topping as Martha set it between them with two spoons.

"Enjoy, you two," she said with a wink.

They ate in silence for a few bites, the warm cinnamon-spiced apples and buttery crumble topping as delicious as Martha had promised.

"So," Beth said after a moment, "tomorrow evening at the church for the volunteer meeting?"

"Yes," Mitch confirmed. "Seven o'clock, I believe."

"And then Thursday evening to set up the outdoor games?"

"Right. I'll bring the camping equipment and anything else we need from the list."

The apple crumble disappeared faster than either expected, each taking careful bites to ensure they didn't overreach their half. When Mitch's spoon clinked against Beth's as they both reached for the last bite, he pulled back.

"You take it," he offered.

"No, you go ahead," Beth insisted.

"How about we split it?" Mitch suggested, dividing the remaining morsel precisely in half with his spoon.

Beth smiled at the gesture. "Perfect solution."

When the check arrived, Mitch reached for it automatically.

"We should split it," Beth said, reaching for her purse. "We're friends planning a church event, after all."

"My treat," Mitch replied gently. "Thanks for helping me figure this out. I was a bit lost on the 'courageous games' front."

After a moment's hesitation, Beth relented with a nod. "Thanks, Mitch. That's very kind."

As they gathered their notes and prepared to leave, the diner had quieted significantly. The dinner rush had ended, leaving just a few regulars nursing coffees and conversations.

"I'll walk you to your car," Mitch offered as they stepped outside into the mild evening air.

"It's behind the boutique," Beth explained.

They walked down the sidewalk and around the corner of Martha's Diner, heading toward the alley that ran behind the Main Street businesses. The shadows had lengthened with the setting sun, but the evening remained bright enough to navigate easily.

"Beautiful evening," Mitch commented as they strolled.

"One of those perfect summer nights," Beth agreed. "Not too hot, not too cool."

They turned down the alley behind the row of shops, their footsteps echoing slightly on the pavement. Beth's car sat alone in the small parking area behind Mountain Chic, bathed in the golden light of early evening.

"Well, I think Pastor Andrew will be impressed with our 'Courageous Trekker' Fun Day plan," Beth said as they reached her vehicle.

"We make a good team," Mitch stated simply.

Beth's expression softened as she looked up at him. "We do. Thanks for dinner, Mitch. This was... fun."

"I enjoyed it. So, I'll see you tomorrow evening at the church for the volunteer meeting?"

"Sounds good."

"Perfect."

Mitch resisted the urge to reach for her hand or extend the evening somehow. Instead, he opened her car door.

"Drive safely," he said as she slid into the driver's seat.

"Always do," Beth replied with a small smile. "Goodnight, Mitch."

"Night, Beth."

He waited until she'd driven away before walking back toward the diner parking lot where his truck was parked. The evening air felt different somehow—fresher, more vibrant—as if the world had taken on a new dimension.

Chapter 12

Beth walked hurriedly, Leslie's laughter trailing behind her, as they rushed toward the recreation hall. They were running five minutes late, a minor miracle considering the train they had gotten stuck waiting on as it passed through town.

"Wait up!" Leslie called. "Not all of us have your gazelle-like legs!"

Beth paused at the recreation hall entrance, her hand on the brass doorknob. "Sorry. I just hate being late."

"It's a church volunteer meeting, not a royal coronation," Leslie teased, finally catching up. "Though I suppose a certain sheriff might be waiting..."

"Leslie!" Beth smoothed the front of her navy blouse and tucked a strand of hair behind her ear. "It's not like that."

"Whatever you say..." Leslie's knowing grin was impossible to deny.

Beth shook her head but couldn't suppress her smile. "Can we just go in? Like normal people attending a normal planning meeting?"

"Lead the way, oh normal one."

The buzz of conversation enveloped them as Beth pulled open the door. About fifteen volunteers sat in chairs arranged in a loose semicircle facing Pastor Andrew and Lily at the front. Beth's gaze instinctively swept the room, landing almost immediately on Mitch. He sat beside Tessa, his posture relaxed but attentive as he listened to something Earl was saying.

Mitch glanced toward the door. His expression brightened, the corners of his eyes crinkling as he nodded a greeting. Something fluttered in Beth's chest—something that had nothing to do with their late arrival and everything to do with that direct, endearing gaze.

"See?" Leslie whispered. "Totally normal."

Tessa spotted them next, waving enthusiastically and pointing to two empty chairs beside her. Beth felt Leslie's gentle nudge at her back, propelling her forward.

"Sorry we're late," Beth apologized quietly as they reached the seats. "We had to wait for a train to pass through, and then traffic in town was really heavy this evening."

"Don't worry, you haven't missed anything," Tessa assured her. "Pastor Andrew was just getting everyone settled."

"Hey... glad you made it," Mitch said as he turned her way.

His voice was low, meant only for her, and Beth felt a warmth bloom in her cheeks. "Me too."

"Now that everyone's here," Pastor Andrew began, clapping his hands together, "let's open in prayer before we dive into our VBS planning."

The rustle of movement subsided as heads bowed. Beth closed her eyes, clasping her hands in her lap.

"Heavenly Father," Pastor Andrew's voice rang clear in the quiet room, "we thank You for bringing us together to serve Your children. Guide our plans for Vacation Bible School, that we might show Your love through our actions and words. Give us wisdom, patience, and joy as we prepare for next week's activities. We ask this in Jesus' name, amen."

A chorus of amens followed as people settled back in their chairs.

"First, I want to thank each of you for volunteering," Pastor Andrew continued. "Our 'Courageous Trekkers' theme is all about finding God's guidance on life's journey, and I'm excited to see how each of you brings this message to life for our children."

Lily stepped forward with a stack of papers. "As you can see by the final schedule each of you were given, we'll have our usual rotation of Bible lessons, crafts, music, and snack time Monday through Thursday. Then Friday is our special Fun Day."

"Which brings me to our outdoor activities," Pastor Andrew added, his enthusiasm evident. "Mitch and Beth have developed a wonderful set of 'Courageous Trekker' games that will really bring our theme home on Friday. Mitch shared the plans with me, and I'm impressed with how you both have tied each activity to a biblical lesson about courage."

Beth caught Mitch's eye, sharing a quick smile of accomplishment. His expression mirrored her pride in their collaborative effort.

"Would either of you like to give everyone a quick overview?" Pastor Andrew asked.

Mitch gestured to Beth. "You want to take this one?"

"Sure." Beth straightened in her chair. "We will have an obstacle course with stations that represent different challenges the Israelites and other biblical figures faced. There's a 'River Jordan' crossing using blue tarps and stepping stones, a 'Mountain Climb' with portable steps, a 'Spider Web' challenge with ropes, and a 'Daniel's Lions' Den' beanbag toss."

"Each station will have a Scripture verse about courage," Mitch added. "And we're setting up a base camp tent where kids can collect stamps on their 'Courage Passports' after completing each challenge."

Martha raised her hand. "What about refreshments for these courageous little explorers? They'll work up quite an appetite."

"We're planning trail mix, fruit skewers, and cookies," Beth explained. "All packaged in little explorer-themed containers."

"Fruit skewers, that's a lot of work," Martha noted. "I'd be happy to come early on Friday to help prepare them. Maybe some watermelon cut into star shapes too—it's been so hot lately."

"That would be wonderful, Martha," Beth said gratefully. "Thank you."

"I'll order the cookies from the bakery in town and bring them on Friday," Leslie offered.

"Perfect!" Pastor Andrew beamed at the group. "This is exactly the kind of teamwork that makes our church family so special."

As Pastor Andrew continued with other details, Beth's attention drifted to Mitch. He sat with one ankle crossed over his knee, his posture attentive yet relaxed. He'd come straight from work, still in his uniform pants and boots, though he'd exchanged his official shirt for a simple navy polo that emphasized his broad shoulders. A day's worth of stubble shadowed his jaw, giving him a slightly rugged appearance that contrasted with his alert, thoughtful expression.

When Lily handed out information packets, Mitch passed one to Beth, their fingers brushing. The brief contact sent a small jolt up her arm—something too strong to dismiss as static electricity. Mitch's eyes met hers for a heartbeat, and Beth wondered if he'd felt it too.

"Now, for setup," Pastor Andrew continued, drawing Beth's attention back to the meeting. "We'll need volunteers on Thursday evening to prepare the outdoor areas. Can I get a show of hands for who's available?"

Beth raised her hand, along with about half the group, including Mitch and Tessa.

"Wonderful," Pastor Andrew noted the names. "Let's plan to meet here at six."

The remainder of the meeting covered logistics—check-in procedures, safety protocols, and snack rotations. Throughout it all, Beth remained acutely aware of Mitch's presence beside her—the subtle scent of his cologne, the way he leaned forward slightly when listening intently, and the occasional nod of agreement that sent a lock of dark hair falling across his forehead.

When Pastor Andrew closed the meeting with a final prayer, the group broke into smaller conversations. Beth gathered her notes, tucking them into her purse.

"So," Mitch turned toward her, his voice dropping slightly to create a pocket of privacy in the bustling room, "Six o'clock tomorrow?"

"Absolutely," Beth confirmed. "I've already started gathering supplies. I found these cute explorer stickers for the Courage Passports at the general store this morning."

"Perfect. I'll bring the camping gear and ropes from my barn."

"And I'll run to the store tomorrow morning and buy blue tarps for the river crossing," Tessa added, leaning into their conversation. "The kids are going to love what you two have planned."

"It's a team effort," Beth said, including Tessa in her smile.

"Beth, are you ready to head out?" Leslie appeared at her side, car keys in hand. "I promised Mom I'd stop by on the way home."

"Of course." Beth gathered her purse. To Mitch, she added, "See you tomorrow at six?"

"I'll be here," he confirmed. "Drive safely."

As Beth and Leslie walked through the parking lot toward Leslie's car, the evening air carried the sweet scent of honeysuckle from the church's garden. Crickets had begun their nightly chorus, their rhythmic chirping a summer soundtrack Beth had loved since childhood.

"Well, that was productive," Leslie observed as they reached her car. "And I don't just mean the VBS planning." She unlocked the doors with a wink.

Beth sighed, though she couldn't suppress her smile. "Leslie…"

"What? He barely took his eyes off you the entire meeting. And you, my dear, were practically glowing every time he spoke to you." Leslie slid into the driver's seat. "'Friends,' my foot."

Beth buckled her seatbelt, considering her response. With anyone else, she might have deflected or changed the subject. But Leslie had been there through the darkest days after Matt left—had seen Beth at her lowest, most broken point. If anyone deserved her honesty now, it was Leslie.

"It's… comfortable. Easy. I'm just enjoying getting to know him," Beth admitted, offering more than she normally would.

Leslie pulled out of the parking lot, her expression softening as she glanced at Beth. "Good. You deserve 'comfortable and easy' after everything." She reached across to squeeze Beth's arm briefly. "And he's a good man, Beth. Strong and gentle… he's one of the good ones. It's evident he knows you're someone special."

Beth gazed out the window at the familiar streets of Laurel Ridge passing by, Leslie's words settling into her heart. "Strong and gentle" did describe Mitch perfectly. Unlike Matt's flashy confidence that had demanded attention, Mitch's quiet strength created space for others to shine.

"I'm not ready to define whatever this is," Beth said after a moment. "But I can't deny there's… something."

"Something good," Leslie affirmed. "Something worth exploring at your own pace. No pressure." She grinned suddenly. "Well, no pressure from me, anyway. I can't speak for Martha."

"Martha is relentless."

"I think she just wants to see you happy again... I know I'm seen more joy in you these past few days."

"Really?"

Leslie stopped at a red light and turned to look at her friend. "When's the last time you smiled this much? Or laughed so easily? Or looked forward to being a part of something outside your store?"

"It's been a while," she admitted.

"Yes, it has." Leslie's tone was triumphant as the light turned green. "And that, my friend, is worth celebrating, regardless of what you're calling it."

They drove in comfortable silence for a few blocks; the streetlights casting intermittent patterns across the dashboard.

"So," Leslie finally asked, her voice casual but her intentions transparent, "what are you wearing tomorrow?"

"Leslie!"

"What? It's a legitimate question. Practical, even. You'll be setting up outdoor games, so you need to be comfortable, but also..."

"But also what?"

"But also, you know, cute." Leslie wiggled her eyebrows.

Beth laughed, the sound filling the car. "You're impossible."

"I'm helpful," Leslie corrected. "And as your best friend, it's my sworn duty to ensure you look fabulous while setting up Bible school obstacle courses with handsome sheriffs."

"Is that in the best friend's handbook?" Beth asked dryly.

"Chapter six, right after, 'Always tell her when she has lipstick on her teeth.'"

Leslie pulled into the parking space behind Beth's store and turned toward her. "I'm really happy for you. Whatever this is, wherever it goes... you deserve it."

The simple sincerity in Leslie's voice touched Beth deeply. "Thanks Leslie... I'm beginning to think I do deserve to be happy."

Chapter 13

Mitch balanced a stack of wooden crates against his hip, squinting against the evening sun as it slanted across the church lawn. Through the busy tangle of volunteers setting up for tomorrow's VBS finale, his gaze found Beth across the grass. She was laughing, head tilted back, one hand braced against Leslie's shoulder as they struggled with a knotted length of thick rope meant for the "spider web" challenge.

The sound carried across the church grounds, light and genuine. A breeze caught her ponytail, lifting it briefly before letting it settle against her neck. She wore faded jeans and a simple green t-shirt that somehow made her eyes more vibrant, even from this distance.

When Pastor Andrew had first mentioned the VBS setup, Mitch had mentally filed it away as another community obligation—important, but ultimately routine. Yet here he stood, finding unexpected pleasure in what should have been just another volunteer duty.

"Must be some view," Reed's voice broke into his thoughts as his deputy helped him position the crates that would become part of their makeshift obstacle course.

Mitch set his crates down, straightening. "Just making sure everyone has what they need."

Reed's knowing glance swept from Mitch to Beth and back again. "Right. Very thorough of you, Sheriff."

"Something you want to say, Dunbar?" Mitch asked, though the slight upturn at the corner of his mouth betrayed him.

Reed arranged the last crate before answering. "Just noting that I've never seen you look so... invested in volunteering before." He paused. "It's a good look on you."

"It's for a good cause," Mitch deflected, though he couldn't quite suppress the small smile forming.

"The cause, huh?" Reed nodded toward Beth, who was now triumphantly holding up the untangled rope. "Not the company?"

Mitch sighed, recognizing the futility of denial. "The company doesn't hurt."

"Thought so." Reed clapped him on the shoulder. "For what it's worth, the whole department thinks she's good for you. Even Jason mentioned it yesterday."

"The whole department is discussing my personal life?" Mitch raised an eyebrow.

"The sheriff suddenly smiling more? That's headline news," Reed grinned.

A commotion drew their attention to the far side of the lawn. One of the large blue tarps meant to represent the River Jordan was catching the evening breeze, billowing upward despite Tessa's attempts to secure one corner. Pastor Andrew and another volunteer scrambled to grab the opposite edges as it threatened to sail away like a massive sail.

Mitch jogged across the lawn, arriving at the same moment as Beth. Her cheeks were flushed from exertion, a few strands of hair escaping her ponytail to frame her face.

"Looks like the River Jordan is trying to become the Sea of Galilee," Beth quipped as they converged on the billowing tarp.

"Or a kite," Mitch added, grabbing the corner nearest him.

With their combined efforts, they managed to subdue the unwieldy blue plastic. Beth knelt beside him, her knee brushing his as they considered the problem.

"We need weights," she said, her breath slightly quickened from the brief struggle. "Or stakes."

"I brought tent pegs," Mitch offered. "They should hold it down if we put enough of them around the perimeter."

"Perfect." Beth tucked a strand of hair behind her ear, inadvertently leaving a smudge of dirt on her cheek from her hand. "We could use some larger rocks, too."

Their heads were close together as they strategized, voices lowered in concentration. The surrounding activity—Leslie calling questions about where to place the finishing touches on the spider web, Pastor Andrew directing volunteers with coolers—faded into background noise.

"So if we put them here, and here," she pointed as she spoke, "the kids can have fun crossing without making it too challenging for the little ones."

"Smart," Mitch nodded, watching her. "We could mark the 'safe' spots with those rubber discs from the rec hall."

Leslie approached, repeating her question more loudly. "Earth to Beth! Passport station?"

Beth looked up, blinking as if emerging from a private conversation. "Sorry, Leslie. We were just figuring out this river situation."

"I can see that. Very... absorbing problem."

Mitch stood, brushing off his jeans. "I'll get those tent pegs from my truck."

As he walked to the parking lot, Mitch glanced back at Beth, who had moved to help Tessa arrange the rubber stepping discs. The easy way she interacted with his sister struck him—warm, genuine, with none of the forced politeness that sometimes characterized people's interactions with the sheriff's family. Tessa laughed at something Beth said, their heads bent together like old friends.

When he returned with the tent pegs, Beth was kneeling beside a teenage volunteer, patiently explaining the concept behind the Courage Passports.

"See, each station has its own stamp," she was saying, demonstrating with a small rubber stamp shaped like a mountain. "When they complete a challenge, they get a stamp on their passport. After they collect all five stamps, they can come to Base Camp for their explorer treats."

The girl nodded, her initial nervousness replaced by enthusiasm. "That's so cool, Ms. Rutledge!"

"Beth, please," she corrected gently. "And it was Mitch's idea to have the Base Camp station. I'm just adding the finishing touches."

Hearing his name from her lips sent a pleasant warmth through him. He approached, holding up the bag of tent pegs. "River Jordan stabilization, as requested."

Beth looked up, her smile brightening. "My hero."

The words were light, teasing, but they settled deep inside him, nonetheless.

Together with Tessa and Pastor Andrew, they secured the tarp to the ground, creating a realistic-looking "river" complete with stepping stones across it. As they worked, Mitch found himself cataloging small details about Beth—the way she bit her lower lip when concentrating, how she instinctively touched the silver pendant at her throat when considering a problem, and the quick efficiency of her movements that spoke of someone accustomed to getting things done.

Her energy radiated outward, touching everyone around her. He hadn't realized how much his life had been running on reserve until Beth's quiet vibrancy started recharging something within him.

"I think that's secure," Beth finally declared, testing the tarp's edge with her foot. "The wind's died down, anyway."

"One biblical flood averted," Mitch quipped, earning a genuine laugh from Beth.

"Let's test the Lions' Den station next," she suggested, pointing to where several volunteers had finished setting up the beanbag toss area. Cardboard cutouts of lions with open mouths served as targets, surrounded by a "den" made from hay bales.

As they crossed the lawn, Mitch felt a peculiar lightness in his step. When was the last time he'd anticipated an evening of volunteer work with such interest? Even mundane tasks felt somehow elevated in Beth's company.

"Ladies first," he offered when they reached the beanbag station.

Beth accepted a small beanbag with mock seriousness. "Daniel, I shall save you from these ferocious beasts."

She tossed the beanbag, missing the lion's mouth by several inches. Her second attempt sailed over the cardboard cutout entirely.

"Okay, maybe my aim needs work if I'm going to save Daniel," she admitted with a self-deprecating smile.

Mitch picked up a beanbag. "Just takes practice." He lined up his shot and tossed it smoothly, landing it directly in the central lion's mouth. "See? Easy."

"Show-off," Beth teased, picking up another beanbag.

"Sheriff's training," he explained with exaggerated seriousness. "Very important life skill."

"I'm sure it comes up all the time in your official duties," she countered, attempting another toss that bounced off the lion's nose.

"You'd be surprised," Mitch replied, handing her another beanbag. "Try standing like this." He demonstrated a better stance.

Beth mimicked his position, her next throw landing squarely in a lion's mouth. "I did it!" she exclaimed, her face lighting up with disproportionate joy for such a small accomplishment.

"At least we know now that I definitely don't have to wear the lion costume," Mitch remarked, remembering their earlier joke at Martha's.

Beth's laughter rang out, clear and unrestrained, hitting him somewhere deep in his chest. "Can you imagine? Sheriff Baker, terror of the biblical beasts."

"The criminals of Laurel Ridge would never fear me again," he said solemnly, though his eyes crinkled with humor.

"I don't know," Beth said, her gaze sweeping over him appreciatively before she seemed to catch herself. "You'd make a pretty imposing lion."

The comment, casual as it was, warmed his face. He cleared his throat. "How's the Base Camp coming along?"

"Almost finished," she replied.

As the evening progressed, most of the major setup was completed. Volunteers began dispersing, some heading home, while others gathered around the coolers for bottled water. Mitch helped Reed and Pastor Andrew secure the last of the equipment, then headed toward the Base Camp tent, where Beth was putting final touches on the display.

She'd transformed the simple pop-up tent into something magical. His old camping lantern hung from the center pole, casting a warm glow over the interior. His well-worn canteen and folded trail maps were artfully arranged alongside colorful explorer-themed items she'd created. A small banner reading "Courageous Trekkers Base Camp" in bright letters was strung across the entrance.

Beth knelt inside, arranging stacks of handmade passports on a small folding table. Each passport was decorated with compass designs and Bible verses about courage. Beside them sat a row of rubber stamps and ink pads.

He ducked into the tent, the enclosed space making him acutely aware of her presence. The scent of her perfume, something light and floral—mingled in the air.

"This looks fantastic, Beth," he said, genuine admiration in his voice. "The kids are going to feel like real adventurers." He pointed to the lantern. "I like how you incorporated my old gear."

She looked up, a pleased but slightly shy smile warming her features. "Thanks. I just wanted it to be special for them. Something to make them feel like they're really on a journey." She adjusted a passport, smoothing its edge with careful fingers.

"It is special," Mitch said, his voice lowering. "You made it special."

Her hand rested on the small table, palm down against the colorful surface. Without fully considering, Mitch gently placed his hand over hers.

Beth's breath caught audibly. Her eyes, wide and startled, met his. In them, he saw surprise, vulnerability, and something warm and receptive that made his heart beat faster. A soft blush colored her cheeks, visible even in the lantern's gentle light.

For a long moment, neither moved. The sounds from outside—Leslie and Tessa laughing, volunteers calling goodbyes—seemed to fade away. She didn't pull her hand away immediately. For several heartbeats, she let it rest beneath him, warm and still.

Then, with a small, almost self-conscious smile, she gently slid her hand from beneath his, her gaze dropping to the passports before lifting back to his face.

"Well, they'll need their official 'Courage Passports' to claim their... uh... 'fearless fruit skewers' tomorrow," she said. Her voice was softer than usual, a touch of lightness returning to break the intensity of the moment.

Mitch felt the slight withdrawal, but understood it completely. It wasn't rejection—it was caution. Patience Baker, he reminded himself. She's worth every bit of it. A wave of protectiveness, tenderness, and determination washed over him.

"Right," he nodded, his smile unwavering. "The very important 'fearless fruit skewers.'"

The tent flap rustled as Leslie poked her head in. "Everything okay here at Base Camp? Looks official enough to launch an expedition."

"Just finishing up," Beth replied, her voice slightly higher than normal.

Tessa joined them, ducking into the increasingly crowded tent. "This looks amazing, Beth!"

"It was a group effort," Beth deflected, standing and brushing off her jeans.

"False modesty," Leslie countered. "This tent was boring canvas before Hurricane Beth blew through it."

As they emerged from the tent, Mitch noted the obstacle course, now fully assembled, waited for tomorrow's excited children. Pastor Andrew walked the perimeter, checking each station with obvious approval.

"I think we've done it," Pastor Andrew called over. "Everything looks perfect for tomorrow's finale. Thank you all for your hard work."

Volunteers began gathering belongings and heading toward the parking lot. Mitch helped fold the last of the extra tarps, stowing them in the church storage shed. When he emerged, he saw Beth saying goodbye to Tessa near the parking lot.

Beth looked up, offering a small wave. He crossed the lawn toward her, reluctant for the evening to end.

"Headed out?" he asked as he approached.

"Yes, I should get home. Big day tomorrow." She tucked a strand of hair behind her ear, the gesture now familiar to him.

"I'll walk you to your car," he offered.

They fell into step together, the gravel of the parking lot crunching beneath their feet. A contemplative silence settled between them, not uncomfortable but charged with unspoken thoughts.

"You're making this whole VBS project something I'm actually looking forward to." Mitch said as they reached her vehicle.

Beth smiled, meeting his gaze more readily now. "It's been fun, Mitch."

"See you tomorrow, then?"

"Wouldn't miss it." She opened her car door. "Goodnight, Mitch."

"Night, Beth. Drive safely."

"Always."

As her car pulled away, he felt a profound sense of rightness and quiet joy.

Chapter 14

Beth handed a colorful fruit skewer to a bright-eyed seven-year-old, whose cheeks were flushed with exertion and excitement. The little boy—Tommy Jenkins, if she remembered correctly—clutched his "Courage Passport" proudly in one hand, all five stamps visible on the small booklet's pages.

"Well done, Courageous Trekker," Beth said, her voice lifting with genuine enthusiasm. "You conquered every challenge!"

Tommy grinned, revealing a gap where his front tooth should have been. "The spider web was the hardest, but Sheriff Baker told me I was brave, like David facing Goliath!"

"He's absolutely right," Beth affirmed, handing him a cookie decorated to look like a compass. "Bravery isn't about not being scared—it's about doing something even when you are scared."

As Tommy skipped away toward his waiting friends, Beth's gaze drifted across the church lawn to where Mitch knelt beside a hesitant little girl at the Mountain Climb station. The child—pigtails drooping slightly in the afternoon heat—shook her head vigorously at whatever

Mitch was suggesting, her small shoulders hunched with apprehension.

Instead of pushing or dismissing her fears, Mitch simply sat cross-legged on the grass beside her, speaking to her. Beth couldn't hear his words, but she watched as the tension gradually left the child's posture. After a moment, the girl nodded, and Mitch offered his hand. Together, they approached the climbing structure, Mitch matching his pace to her tentative steps.

The gentleness in his interaction struck Beth deeply. This wasn't Sheriff Baker enforcing rules or maintaining order—this was just Mitch, patient and understanding, his deep laugh carrying across the church grounds as the little girl successfully reached the top of the wooden structure.

The navy t-shirt he wore—Courageous Trekkers emblazoned across the back—stretched slightly across his shoulders as he raised his arms to high-five the triumphant children. A lock of dark hair fell across his forehead when he bent to help her back down.

"Well now, isn't that something nice to see?" Martha's voice broke into her thoughts. The older woman arranged a fresh tray of "Brave Banana" slices beside the lemonade dispenser, her knowing eyes following Beth's gaze. "Our Sheriff has a way with children."

"He's good with them," Beth acknowledged, arranging more fruit skewers on the display tray. "Natural, even."

"Always has been," Martha replied, refilling a small paper cup with lemonade for a thirsty child who approached the table.

Beth watched as Mitch demonstrated the proper throwing technique at the beanbag station, his movements both confident and relaxed. There was something undeniably attractive about seeing this side of him—unguarded, playful. The serious lines of responsibility temporarily softened around his eyes.

He's so different from the reserved sheriff who first walked into my boutique, Beth thought. *I'm seeing parts of him that he usually keeps hidden.*

An unbidden comparison to Matt flashed through her mind—how her ex-husband's charm had always seemed calculated for maximum effect, a performance meant to impress whoever was watching. Mitch's kindness, by contrast, seemed woven into the very fabric of who he was, displayed without thought of audience or reward.

The realization brought both warmth and a prickle of unease. Could this be real? Or am I just setting myself up for another fall?

"You're going to wear a hole through him with all that staring, you know," Leslie teased, appearing at Beth's side with a fresh container of cookies from the church kitchen.

Beth felt heat rise to her cheeks. "I wasn't staring. I was... supervising."

"Mm-hmm," Leslie hummed, unconvinced. "Very thorough supervision. Especially of one particular volunteer."

Martha chimed in from beside the lemonade dispenser, wiping condensation from the plastic container with a checkered dish towel. "Go on, child. We've got this handled. Looks like Mitch could use a partner for that 'River Jordan' crossing, and these old legs aren't up for it." She punctuated the suggestion with an exaggerated wink that made Beth both blush and laugh.

"Oh, I don't know..." Beth hedged, glancing at the trays of remaining refreshments. "I should help here..."

Leslie handed her a bottle of water from the cooler. "Go. Have some fun. You deserve it. Besides, your 'planning partner' might appreciate the company."

Beth hesitated, feeling the familiar pull of responsibility warring with the stronger, newer pull toward Mitch. The memory of their easy collaboration planning this event—the shared laughter, the natural way their ideas had complemented each other—tipped the scales.

When was the last time I just... played? She wondered. The question brought no immediate answer, which was answer enough.

"Okay," she relented with a smile, "but if you run out of 'Brave Bananas,' don't blame me."

"Honey, we've got enough bananas to feed a troop of monkeys," Martha assured her. "Now go on before I shoo you with this dish towel."

Beth walked across the church lawn, navigating around excited children racing between stations and parent volunteers. The summer air hummed with laughter and shouts of triumph as young "trekkers" conquered each biblical challenge.

Mitch was at the edge of the obstacle course, patiently untangling a section of rope that had become knotted during enthusiastic use. A small boy waited nearby, bouncing on the balls of his feet with barely contained energy.

"Need an extra pair of hands?" Beth asked as she approached.

Mitch looked up, his concentration breaking into a wide smile that crinkled the corners of his eyes and sent an unexpected flutter through Beth's chest.

"Always," he replied, "especially when it comes to rogue ropes and enthusiastic trekkers." He gestured toward the various stations where children raced about. "Things are going well, thanks to our brilliant planning."

"Brilliant is a strong word," Beth demurred, taking the other end of the rope to help with the knot. "But I think the kids are having fun."

"Think we're too old to try the Spider Web ourselves?" Mitch asked, a playful challenge in his voice as the knot finally came loose.

"Or maybe help that group over there figure out the beanbag toss technique?"

Beth glanced at the small cluster of children struggling to hit the lion targets. "I think my disastrous performance yesterday qualifies me as the perfect person to teach them what not to do."

"Perfect. Show them the wrong way, and I'll demonstrate the right way." His eyes sparked with good-natured teasing. "Unless you've miraculously improved overnight."

"Fighting words, Sheriff," Beth replied, surprising herself with the ease of their banter. "Lead on."

They approached the beanbag station, where several children were taking turns attempting to land beanbags in the cardboard lions' mouths. Most throws fell short or flew wide, resulting in groans of disappointment.

"Looking good, explorers," Mitch encouraged, "but I think we might have a technique that could help. Ms. Beth and I are going to demonstrate."

"Ms. Beth is going to show you what happens when you throw like this," Beth said, deliberately positioning her feet too close together and hunching her shoulders. Her throw sailed dramatically wide off the target, earning giggles from the children.

"And Sheriff Baker will show you the right way," she added, stepping back with an exaggerated bow.

Mitch demonstrated the proper stance and technique, his movements fluid and precise. The beanbag landed squarely in the central lion's mouth, eliciting impressed "oohs" from their young audience.

"Now, the key is planting your feet about shoulder-width apart," Mitch explained, kneeling down to help a small girl adjust her stance. "And follow through with your arm, like you're reaching toward the target."

Beth moved among the children, gently correcting grips and encouraging each attempt. "That's it, Zoey! Much closer this time!"

When her turn came around again, Beth concentrated on applying Mitch's advice. Her throw arced through the air and landed directly in a lion's mouth, surprising even herself.

"Look at that!" Mitch exclaimed, genuine pride in his voice. "Perfect shot."

"I had a good teacher," Beth acknowledged, warmth spreading through her at his praise.

They moved next to the River Jordan crossing, where a group of younger children needed help to navigate the blue tarp "river" with its stepping-stone path. Beth took one little boy's hand while Mitch steadied a pigtailed girl on his other side.

"One step at a time," Beth encouraged, feeling the small, sticky hand clutch hers tightly. "Just like Joshua led the Israelites across the Jordan, we're going to cross together."

"Were the Israelites scared?" the little boy asked, his voice small as he eyed the expanse of blue tarp before them.

"I think they might have been," Beth answered honestly. "But God promised to be with them, just like He's with you. And look—you've got me on one side and Sheriff Baker on the other."

"And we won't let you fall," Mitch added, his reassurance directed at both children, but his warm gaze meeting Beth's over their heads.

The shared purpose, the simple joy of helping these children overcome their fears, resonated deeply within Beth. This easy partnership felt so natural, as if they'd been working side by side for years instead of days.

As the afternoon progressed, Beth completely immersed herself in the games and activities, her earlier self-consciousness forgotten. She cheered as children completed each challenge, helped reset stations between groups, and even took a turn scrambling through the Spider Web obstacle herself when a particularly shy boy refused to try it without an adult going first.

Throughout it all, she remained aware of Mitch's presence—his laugh mixing with the children's, the brief touches as they passed supplies or steadied the same child, the way his gaze found hers across the lawn, carrying shared amusement or pride in a particular child's accomplishment.

"Ms. Beth! Watch me!" called Emma Henderson, Dorothy's granddaughter, as she prepared to toss a beanbag.

Beth turned to offer encouragement, but her words died in her throat as Emma's enthusiastic throw went dramatically off-course—heading straight for Pastor Andrew's head as he bent to tie a child's shoelace nearby.

"Pastor, look out!" Beth called, but too late.

The beanbag bounced harmlessly off the pastor's shoulder, causing him to look up in surprise. After a moment of startled silence, he laughed good-naturedly.

"I see Daniel's lions are getting creative with their attacks," he joked, picking up the beanbag and returning it to a mortified Emma.

"I'm sorry, Pastor Andrew," the little girl whispered, her face flaming.

"No harm done," he assured her. "But maybe aim a little lower next time? Lions don't usually perch on people's heads."

The gentle humor diffused the moment, and Emma's smile returned as she lined up for another throw.

"Crisis averted," Mitch murmured, suddenly beside Beth. "Though, for a second there, I thought we might need to add 'First Aid Station' to our obstacle course."

Beth's laughter bubbled up, unrehearsed and genuine. "Can you imagine? 'Welcome to the Good Samaritan Healing Tent—Band-Aids and ice packs for courageous but clumsy trekkers.'"

"I think that's actually in the sheriff's handbook—Chapter Six: 'Church Functions and Their Hidden Dangers.'"

Their shared laughter drew curious glances from nearby parents, but Beth found she didn't mind. The weight she'd carried since Matt's betrayal—the constant vigilance against judgment, the careful maintenance of her independent image—seemed temporarily lifted in these simple moments of connection.

As the afternoon began to wane, parents started arriving to collect their children. The atmosphere shifted from active play to excited recounting of adventures as little ones proudly displayed their completed "Courage Passports" and prizes.

Volunteers began the initial stages of cleanup, collecting stray beanbags and straightening equipment. Beth stood with Mitch near the Base Camp tent, watching as Martha and Leslie handed out the last few stamps and refreshments to stragglers.

"Well," Mitch said, stretching slightly to ease muscles that had spent hours bending to child-height, "I think Operation Courageous Trekkers was a success."

Beth nodded, a contented smile settling on her face as she surveyed the joyful chaos of departing families. "The kids had a blast. And so did I."

"Me too," Mitch admitted, his voice lowering slightly as he turned toward her. "More than I expected."

The sincerity in his tone drew Beth's gaze to his face. The afternoon sun caught the flecks of amber in his brown eyes, warming them to the color of rich maple syrup. There was something in his expression—a quiet intensity beneath the casual words—that quickened her breathing.

"Ready for our breakfast date tomorrow morning?" he asked, his voice casual but his eyes watchful. "Or will you be too tired after all this excitement?"

Beth stilled, the single word echoing in her mind. Date. Not "breakfast as friends" or their usual careful phrasing, but simply, straightforwardly—date.

"A date?" she asked, the question emerging slightly breathless. "Is that what... is that what it is?"

Her mind raced, excitement warring with a sudden surge of her old anxieties. *A date? He thinks of it as a date? What do I think of it as?*

Mitch held her gaze, his expression open and steady. No retreating, no backpedaling to safer ground. Instead, he asked simply, "Do you want it to be?"

The question hung between them, gentle but direct, impossible to evade. Beth found herself at a crossroads she hadn't expected reaching so soon.

Do I want it to be a date?

Her heart answered with a resounding yes—a yes that frightened her with its certainty. But her head, filled with memories of Matt's betrayal and all the warning signs she'd missed, screamed caution.

She looked at Mitch—at his kind eyes that noticed details others missed, at his steady presence that never demanded or presumed, at the way he made her feel simultaneously safe and wonderfully alive. This wasn't Matt. This wasn't the same situation, the same risk.

This was Mitch, who showed up when he said he would. Who listened more than he spoke. Who saw her strength without being threatened by it. Who made her laugh without making anyone else the punchline.

What do I want? The question hung in her mind, accompanied by another, more challenging one: And am I brave enough to admit it, even to myself?

After a Vacation Bible School focused on courage, it seemed fitting that she now faced a test of her own. Not crossing a pretend river or climbing a makeshift mountain, but something far more daunting—trusting her heart again after it had been so thoroughly broken.

"A date... yes... that sounds good."

Chapter 15

Mitch drummed his fingers on the diner table, watching steam rise from his mug of black coffee. The word "date" still echoed in his mind from yesterday, rolling around like a coin that hadn't quite settled. He'd said it without planning to, the term slipping out naturally after carefully avoiding it. And Beth had agreed.

He took a sip of coffee, the rich bitterness grounding him in the present moment as Martha's Diner hummed with its usual Saturday morning activity. The clatter of dishes from the kitchen mingled with fragments of conversation from the scattered breakfast crowd.

"Refill, Sheriff?" Martha appeared at his side, coffeepot in hand.

"Please." He pushed his mug toward her. "Though I might be over caffeinated already."

Martha filled his cup, her knowing eyes taking in his freshly pressed uniform and the way he kept glancing toward the door. "Nervous energy, I'd say. Reminds me of when my Scottie used to take me dancing. Always jittery beforehand, that man."

"I feel like I'm sixteen again," Mitch admitted, surprising himself with the confession. "Ridiculous at my age."

Martha set the coffeepot on the table and slid into the seat across from him, her expression softening. "Age has nothing to do with it. When your heart starts beating for someone special, you're always sixteen inside, whether you're twenty or eighty."

"Is that your professional wisdom as our local matchmaker?" he asked, the corner of his mouth lifting.

"That's my professional wisdom as someone who was married for forty-two years to a man who made my heart skip right until the day he passed." She patted his hand. "The day that feeling stops is the day you should worry, not the other way around."

The bell above Martha's door jingled, drawing Mitch's attention immediately. Beth stood in the entrance, sunlight from the doorway casting her in silhouette for a moment before she stepped fully inside. She wore workout clothes—coral capris and a fitted gray t-shirt—with her blonde hair pulled back in a ponytail. Her face brightened when she spotted him, though he noticed a slight hesitation in her step as she approached.

Martha slid out of the booth with a wink. "And that's my cue. Your usual, Beth honey?"

"Morning," Beth said, sliding into the seat Martha had vacated. "And yes, please."

"Morning, Beth," Mitch replied, a genuine smile spreading across his face. "You look ready for action."

"Meeting Leslie for a hike after breakfast," she explained, settling into the booth. "We try to tackle the Ridge Trail once a week." She eyed his uniform. "Working today, I see?"

"Shift starts at nine. Saturday mornings are usually quiet, though."

Martha returned with Beth's coffee and took their orders—oatmeal with berries for Beth, a side of bacon, to accompany Mitch's coffee.

When Martha moved away, Beth stirred her coffee, adding cream from the small metal pitcher on the table. The soft clink of her spoon against the ceramic filled the momentary quiet.

"Mitch," she said finally, looking up to meet his gaze directly. "About yesterday. When you called this a date..." She paused, her fingers tightening almost imperceptibly around her mug. "What exactly is this? Between us?"

The directness of her question surprised him, though perhaps it shouldn't have. Beth had never been one to dance around important matters. It was one of the things he'd come to admire about her.

He set his coffee mug down, considering his response carefully. He met her gaze steadily. "Maybe the better question is, what do you want it to be, Beth? And do we need to define it right now?"

Beth's expression softened. "I don't know," she admitted. "I feel like I'm re-learning how to date at thirty-four, which is ridiculous."

"Join the club," Mitch said with a small smile. "Dating has never been my strong suit."

"That's hard to believe," she said, raising an eyebrow.

"Believe it. When most of the young guys were figuring out dating, I was busy making sure Tessa and Cody had clean clothes and their homework was done."

Beth nodded, understanding in her eyes. "I guess we're both a little out of practice, then."

"Completely out of practice," he corrected. "But I know that I enjoy being with you, and I'd like to keep doing that. Without the 'just friends' qualifier, if that's something you want to."

Their breakfast arrived, creating a brief pause in the conversation. Martha set down Beth's oatmeal, topped with a generous handful of fresh berries, and Mitch's plate of bacon. She refilled their coffee cups without comment, though her smile spoke volumes.

When she'd gone, Beth took a deep breath. "I enjoy being with you too, Mitch. More than with anyone in a long time." Her voice lowered slightly, as if sharing a secret. "And I'm curious. About what this—we—could be."

The simple admission warmed him more than the coffee ever could.

"But I need to be honest with you," she continued, stirring her oatmeal. "There's a reason I've been so cautious."

"Matt," Mitch supplied quietly.

Beth nodded, her expression growing more serious. "Not just his affair, though that was bad enough. It was..." She hesitated, seeming to gather her thoughts. "Matt had a way of making everything seem like things were always my fault. If his business struggled, it was because I was too focused on my boutique. If he was unhappy, it was because I wasn't attentive enough. If I succeeded at something, it somehow threatened him."

Mitch listened intently, his food forgotten, as Beth continued.

"He started small—little comments about my decisions, suggestions that became criticisms. By the time I realized what was happening, I'd started doubting everything about myself." Her voice remained steady, but Mitch could hear the pain beneath the composure. "I promised myself I'd never be in a relationship like that again, where I lose myself piece by piece."

"That explains a lot," Mitch said softly. "About why you rebuilt everything around independence."

Beth nodded, taking a sip of her coffee. "When I discovered the affair, it was actually almost a relief. I told him to leave... and he did." She looked up, meeting his gaze directly. "But he left me with serious trust issues—not just in others, but in my judgment. If I could be so wrong about someone I married, how could I trust my feelings again?"

The vulnerability in her admission struck Mitch deeply. He understood what it had cost her to share this, to lay bare her fears.

"Thank you for telling me," he said finally. "For trusting me with that."

"I want to be upfront about my baggage," she replied with a small, self-deprecating smile. "It seems only fair."

"We all have baggage, Beth." He considered his next words carefully. "I've never been good at relationships because I've never really prioritized them. Between raising Tessa and Cody, and then focusing on my career, it was easier to keep people at a distance. Safer."

"Safer," she echoed, understanding in her eyes.

"But I know this," Mitch continued, his voice low but clear. "I'm falling for you, Beth. Hard." The admission made his heart pound, but he pressed on. "Being with you makes me feel things I've never allowed myself to feel—good things."

A faint blush colored her cheeks, but she didn't look away.

"I'm not Matt," he said firmly. "I don't want to control you or dim your light. Just the opposite—I want to see you shine. I want to see you thrive and grow." He paused, realizing how much he was revealing, but found he didn't want to stop. "I think God put you in my path for a reason, Beth. And I'm grateful for that every day."

Beth blinked rapidly, a single tear escaping despite her obvious attempt to contain it. She brushed it away quickly. "Mitch, that's... a lot. In a good way." Her voice wavered slightly. "I'm still scared. But I want to see where this goes. With you."

Relief and joy mingled in his chest, nearly overwhelming in their intensity. "One day at a time?" he suggested.

"One day at a time," she agreed. "And with a lot of honesty."

"Always," he promised.

The tension that had hung between them eased, replaced by something gentler—a shared understanding, a beginning. Beth took a bite of her oatmeal, now slightly cooled, and Mitch reached for his bacon.

"So," Beth said after a moment, her tone lighter, "what does Sheriff Baker do on his Saturdays, when he's not working or having breakfast with boutique owners?"

"Depends on the Saturday," Mitch replied, grateful for the shift to easier conversation. "Sometimes I help Earl with deliveries at the hardware store. I've been fixing up the barn at home—the roof needs patching before winter. And there's usually some paperwork waiting at the office if I'm extremely bored."

"Sounds thrilling," Beth teased.

"Not exactly the stuff of adventure novels," he admitted with a smile. "What about you? Besides mountain climbing with Leslie, I mean."

"It's hardly mountain climbing. More like a vigorous walk uphill and a welcome cooldown when we walk back down." Beth took another bite of oatmeal. "Saturdays are usually for errands, catching up on boutique paperwork, maybe some reading. Pretty mundane too."

"Nothing wrong with mundane," Mitch said. "Sometimes mundane is exactly what a person needs."

Beth tilted her head, studying him. "You know, most people are trying to escape the mundane. They want excitement, adventure."

"I get enough excitement and adventure during work hours," Mitch replied honestly. "There's something to be said for quiet Saturday mornings with a good cup of coffee."

"Mundane is pretty appealing," Beth said softly.

They finished breakfast as conversation flowed between them. Beth described the potential children's boutique space. She was pretty sure she would sign the contract to lease the space this week, her excitement evident as she outlined her vision. Mitch listened attentively, asking questions that showed genuine interest.

"What time are you meeting Leslie today?" he asked as they finished the last of their coffee.

Beth glanced at her watch. "Fifteen minutes. We're meeting at the trailhead." She hesitated. "Will I see you tomorrow? At church?"

"I'll be there, and I'll save you a seat," Mitch confirmed. "Maybe we could grab lunch afterward? The weather's supposed to be nice—we could pick up sandwiches from the deli and find a spot in the park."

"I'd like that," Beth said, her smile warm. "It's a date. An actual, official date."

"Second date," Mitch corrected with a grin, gesturing to their empty plates.

"So it is," Beth acknowledged, her eyes bright. "I should get going. Leslie will be waiting, and she gets cranky if she has to delay her endorphin rush."

Mitch stood as Beth gathered her purse, leaving enough cash on the table to cover both their meals, despite her protests. They walked together to the door, Mitch holding it open for her.

Outside, the morning sun had climbed higher, warming the sidewalks of Main Street. A few shops were already open, their doors propped wide to welcome weekend customers. The scent of fresh bread from the bakery mingled with the lingering aroma of Martha's coffee as they paused on the sidewalk.

"Thank you for being honest with me," Mitch replied. "It means a lot, Beth."

An unexpected boldness seized him. Before he could overthink it, Mitch leaned down and pressed a gentle kiss to Beth's cheek. Her skin was soft beneath his lips, and he caught the subtle scent of her shampoo—something floral and fresh. He pulled back slightly, gauging her reaction.

Beth's eyes widened in surprise, but the smile that followed was genuine. "What was that for?"

"Because I've been wanting to do that," Mitch admitted. "And because a first date should end with at least a kiss on the cheek."

"Well, in that case," Beth said, her voice slightly breathless, "our first date has officially ended properly."

"I'll see you tomorrow," Mitch said, reluctant to part but aware of both her waiting friend and his upcoming shift.

"Tomorrow," Beth confirmed. She started to turn, then paused, looking back at him with an expression that made his breath catch. "Have a good day, Mitch. Be safe out there."

"Always am," he replied, their familiar exchange carrying new weight.

He watched her walk away, the morning sunlight catching in her blonde ponytail. Only when she turned the corner did he head toward his truck, a smile lingering on his face. The word "date" still echoed in his mind, but now it had settled into place, solid and real and full of promise.

Chapter 16

Beth swerved into the last available spot at the trailhead, gravel crunching beneath her tires as she braked a bit too hard. Glancing at the dashboard clock—8:45 AM—she winced. Late. Not terribly, but Leslie was punctual to a fault when it came to their Saturday hikes.

She spotted her friend, leaning against her car, water bottle in hand, surveying the modest collection of hikers preparing to tackle the trails. Leslie's bright pink athletic outfit made her impossible to miss against the backdrop of earthy greens and browns.

The morning sun filtered through the canopy of oak and maple trees, creating an ever-shifting pattern of light and shadow across the parking area. Beth took a deep breath, trying to settle the jumble of emotions that had followed her after breakfast—Mitch's words echoing in her mind: *I'm falling for you, Beth. Hard.*

As she stepped out of her car, adjusting her ponytail and grabbing her small backpack, Leslie pushed away from her vehicle with an exaggerated checking of her non-existent watch.

"Look what the cat dragged in! Or, in this case, what a certain handsome sheriff finally let out of his sight," Leslie called, a knowing smirk spreading across her face.

Beth rolled her eyes, though she couldn't quite suppress the smile tugging at her lips. "Good morning to you, too."

"Oh, it certainly looks like it was." Leslie waggled her eyebrows. "Spill it—what's got you fifteen minutes late and looking like you've just swallowed the canary?"

"I don't look like anything."

"Honey, your cheeks are pinker than my outfit, and you've got that glazed look you get when you find the perfect merchandise for the boutique—except multiplied by about a thousand."

Beth shouldered her backpack, deliberately avoiding Leslie's inquisitive gaze. "Are we hiking or conducting an interrogation?"

"Both, obviously." Leslie grinned, falling into step beside Beth as they headed toward the trailhead marker. "Multitasking is my superpower."

The trail stretched before them, a winding path that climbed steadily through dense woodland before opening to spectacular valley views at several strategic outlooks. They'd hiked it countless times over the years, in all seasons and weathers. Today, the trail beckoned with summer splendor—wildflowers dotting the edges, birds calling from the branches above, and the earthy scent of soil and vegetation rich in the morning air.

Their footfalls created a steady rhythm against the packed dirt path. For several minutes, they hiked in silence, the physical exertion providing a welcome outlet for Beth's restless energy.

As they rounded the first significant bend, the trail narrowed and steepened. Beth's foot caught on an exposed root, and she stumbled forward, catching herself just before taking a complete tumble.

"Whoa there!" Leslie grabbed her elbow, steadying her. "You okay?"

"Fine. Just clumsy this morning."

Leslie stopped, planting her hands on her hips. "Alright, out with it. You're quieter than a church mouse during sermon notes, and you almost tripped over a root a five-year-old could spot. Spill. Sheriff-related, I presume?"

Beth adjusted her ponytail again, a nervous habit. "I'm just tired. Long week at the boutique."

"Nice try." Leslie crossed her arms. "The only thing you're tired of is overthinking, and I'm your official overthinking-decipherer. Now, are you going to tell me what's going on, or do I need to start guessing? Because my guesses will get progressively more ridiculous and possibly involve elopement scenarios."

Beth snorted despite herself. "You're impossible."

"Part of my charm. Now talk."

They continued hiking; the path widening slightly as they moved deeper into the woods. The morning light speckled through the leaves overhead, creating shifting patterns on the trail before them. A woodpecker's rhythmic tapping echoed from somewhere to their right.

"It's nothing earth-shattering," Beth hedged, stepping carefully over a fallen branch.

"Beth Rutledge, I have known you since you wore braces and cried over Aaron Thompson, taking Susie Miller to the eighth-grade dance. I can tell when 'nothing earth-shattering' is actually 'my entire emotional landscape is shifting.'"

They reached a small clearing where the trail widened, a couple of large rocks providing natural seating. Leslie stopped, uncapping her water bottle and taking a long drink before fixing Beth with an expectant look.

Beth sighed, relenting. "It's Mitch."

"Shocking," Leslie deadpanned.

"He called our breakfast this morning a 'date,'" Beth continued, the word still feeling strange on her tongue. "An actual date. Not 'friends having breakfast' or whatever we've been calling it."

Leslie's expression softened into genuine interest. "And how did that make you feel?"

Beth unzipped her backpack, pulling out her water bottle, mostly to have something to do with her hands. "Terrified. Excited. Confused." She took a small sip. "All the above?"

"All perfectly reasonable reactions," Leslie nodded. "And what did you say when he dropped the d-word?"

"This morning I asked him what exactly we were doing. What this was between us?" Beth leaned against one of the rocks, feeling the cool, rough surface through her thin, athletic shirt. "I can't believe I was so direct."

"I'm proud of you," Leslie said without a hint of teasing. "That took courage. What did he say?"

Beth's fingers traced the condensation on her water bottle. "He asked what I wanted it to be. If we needed to define it right now."

"Smart man."

"Then he told me he's falling for me." The words came out in a rush, as if saying them quickly might make them less overwhelming. "That he enjoys being with me and wants to keep doing that without the 'just friends' qualifier."

Leslie's eyes widened. "Wow. That's... direct."

"I know."

"And?"

"And I told him I enjoy being with him, too. That I'm curious about what we could be." Beth's voice dropped. "But I also told him about Matt. Not everything, but... enough."

Leslie's expression grew serious. She moved to sit beside Beth on the rock. "That couldn't have been easy."

"It wasn't." Beth stared at the trail ahead, memories surfacing like debris after a storm. "I really, really like him, Les. More than I thought, I was capable of liking anyone again. But it feels so fast. And honestly, how does a thirty-four-year-old woman even 'date' anymore? It feels... foreign."

Leslie bumped her shoulder gently against Beth's. "I don't think there's an age limit on awkward dating experiences. Pretty sure it's universally weird at any age."

A small laugh escaped Beth. "Maybe." Her expression sobered. "What if I mess this up? We've built this nice... ease. What if trying for more ruins, even the friendship?"

"Is that what you're really worried about?" Leslie asked quietly. "The friendship?"

Beth closed her eyes briefly, the real fear rising to the surface. "The biggest thing is... Matt." Her voice caught slightly. "He didn't just break my heart, Les. He made me doubt every instinct I had. I chose him. I built a life with him. And I was so, so wrong." She turned to face her friend, vulnerability etched across her features. "How do I know I'm not making another colossal mistake? How do I trust my feelings when they led me so astray before?"

Leslie's usual playfulness vanished completely. She reached over and took Beth's hand, squeezing it tightly. "Oh, honey. Of course, you're scared. Anyone would be after what that weasel put you through."

"I feel ridiculous even saying it out loud," Beth admitted. "Like I'm fifteen instead of thirty-four."

"As for dating at thirty-four?" Leslie offered a gentle smile. "It's like riding a very wobbly bicycle downhill after a ten-year hiatus. Terrifying, possibly messy, but you might just find you remember how."

That drew a genuine laugh from Beth. They stood and resumed walking, the trail beginning its upward climb toward the first ridge overlook.

"Seriously, though," Leslie continued after a moment, "is there a timeline on these things? God's timing is rarely our own, you know that. If it feels right in your spirit, maybe 'soon' is just 'right on time.'"

Beth considered this, the path beneath her feet growing steeper. "Maybe. But what about ruining what we already have?"

"The best relationships often start as great friendships. And let's be honest, the way he looks at you? I think the 'just friends' ship sailed somewhere around the VBS setup."

They hiked in silence for several minutes, the exertion of the climb requiring their focus. Bird calls punctuated the quiet—a cardinal's clear whistle, the chattering of chickadees, the distant caw of a crow. The forest air grew richer as the sun warmed the canopy above, releasing the scent of pine and summer vegetation.

As they reached a small plateau, both women paused to catch their breath. The view had opened slightly, offering glimpses of the valley below through breaks in the trees.

"Matt wasn't a reflection of your worth or your judgment, Beth," Leslie said suddenly, her voice gentle but firm. "He was a reflection of his brokenness. You're not the same person you were then. You're stronger and wiser. And Mitch? He's a good man. A see-through good man. Not a hint of Matt's manipulative charm anywhere near him."

Beth felt a small knot in her chest loosen at Leslie's words. "How are you so sure?"

"Because I have eyes," Leslie replied simply. "The way Mitch treats you—treats everyone, really—it's with genuine respect. He doesn't need to be the center of attention. He doesn't diminish others to make himself look better." She adjusted her backpack straps. "Remember what Pastor Andrew's sermon was about last week? 'Courage to begin again.' Maybe this is your 'begin again' moment, Beth."

The trail narrowed again as they continued upward, requiring them to walk single file for a stretch. The physical separation gave Beth a moment to absorb Leslie's words.

"It takes courage to open your heart, especially when it's been hurt," Leslie continued when the path widened again. "But isn't that what faith is about, too? Stepping out even when you can't see the whole path? Pray about it. Ask for discernment. God doesn't want you to live in fear."

"'For God has not given us a spirit of fear, but of power and of love and of a sound mind,'" Beth quoted softly.

"Exactly. Second Timothy, right?"

Beth nodded. "My grandmother used to quote that to me whenever I was afraid of trying something new."

They rounded a final bend, and the trail opened suddenly onto the first major overlook—a flat, rocky outcropping that offered a panoramic view of Laurel Ridge Valley. The town itself was visible in the distance, nestled among rolling hills with the silver ribbon of the New River winding alongside it. The mountains rose beyond, blue-hazed and majestic against the clear summer sky.

Both women stopped to drink in the view. The morning sun had risen higher now, illuminating the valley in warm light. A red-tailed hawk circled lazily on thermals rising from the warmed earth below.

"It never gets old, does it?" Leslie murmured.

"Never," Beth agreed, feeling a familiar peace settle over her at the expansive vista.

They found seats on the smooth rocks at the edge of the overlook, legs dangling over the drop. For several minutes, they sat, sipping water and absorbing the natural beauty spread before them.

Beth's thoughts turned inward, processing Leslie's insights. The perspective from this height seemed to mirror her emotional state—seeing things from a different angle often revealed truths that weren't visible from ground level.

"You're right," she said finally, breaking the contemplative silence. "I can't let Matt dictate my future happiness from the past. It's just... it's still so raw sometimes." She took a deep breath. "But Mitch... he makes me feel... hopeful. And maybe hope is worth the risk."

Leslie bumped her shoulder gently. "Atta girl! Hope is always worth the risk. And I am rooting for you. So is Martha. And probably half town."

"Only half?" Beth raised an eyebrow.

"The other half hasn't seen you two together yet. Give it time."

They shared a laugh that echoed briefly across the valley before being swallowed by the vastness of the view. Beth felt lighter, as if sharing her fears had diminished their power. The knot of anxiety that had accompanied her excitement all morning had loosened, not completely undone, but no longer quite so constricting.

"So," Leslie said after they'd savored the view a while longer, "should we tackle the upper ridge, or head back?"

Beth considered, suddenly aware of a vibrant energy replacing her earlier nervous tension. "Let's go all the way up today. I'm feeling... strong."

Leslie's answering smile was knowing. "That's what happens when you stop carrying everything alone, you know. More energy for the climb."

They gathered their belongings and set off again; the trail growing steeper and more challenging as it wound toward the upper ridgeline. Beth found herself moving with more confidence, even on the tricky sections where loose rocks made footing uncertain.

As they continued upward, Beth found her thoughts turning toward tomorrow's lunch with Mitch. A second date. The label no longer felt quite so terrifying. Instead, it carried a sense of possibility, of potential.

Maybe... just maybe... this could be something good, she thought, her steps growing lighter with each foot of elevation gained. The mountain air filled her lungs, clean and refreshing. Ahead, the trail beckoned, challenging but navigable. One step at a time. Just like everything else worth doing.

Beth felt genuinely hopeful about what—and who—waited around the next bend in her life's trail.

Chapter 17

Mitch rocked gently on the porch swing, the wood creaking beneath him like a muted conversation between old friends. Duke's head rested heavily on his boot, the dog's occasional sighs punctuating the evening quiet. A half-empty glass of sweet tea sweated onto the small wicker table beside him, leaving a dark ring next to the mostly demolished box of pizza.

The western sky was a canvas of bruised purple and soft orange as the sun finally dipped below the treeline.

His mind drifted back to breakfast with Beth. Her courage in sharing her past with Matt, the raw honesty in her eyes when she'd admitted her fears. One day at a time. The phrase felt right, steady. The brief, soft press of his lips to her cheek that morning—a small act of boldness that still lingered in his memory.

The screen door creaked open, followed by Cody's footsteps across the wooden porch.

"Thought I smelled the last rites of a pepperoni pizza," Cody said, eyeing the box. "You didn't leave me just the crusts, did you, old man?"

There was an ease to Cody's voice that hadn't been there when he'd first returned to Laurel Ridge—a man settling into his skin rather than a restless soul looking for the next escape route.

Mitch nudged the box toward his brother. "Two slices left. I saved them for you."

"Miracles do happen." Cody grabbed the pizza, refilled his glass of tea from the pitcher, and sank into the adjacent rocking chair. "Man, nothing beats a Saturday evening on this porch."

Cody's expression was content as he stretched his long legs out before him, crossing them at the ankles in a mirror of Mitch's posture.

"Tessa's out on a date," Mitch said.

Cody snorted. "You mean her 'coffee meeting' with the new youth pastor? The one she spent two hours getting ready for?"

"That would be the one."

"Hope he knows what he's getting into," Cody grinned. "Tess texted me about twenty minutes ago. Just a thumbs-up emoji. I'm taking that as a positive sign."

The rhythmic chirp of crickets rose around them, starting their nightly concert. From a neighboring farm came the distant, mournful moo of a cow. The air carried the metallic tang of evening cooling, along with the scent of pine from the woods bordering their yard, mingling with the lingering aroma of pizza.

Duke raised his head briefly, ears perking at some sound beyond human hearing, before settling back down with a heavy sigh.

"Lazy mutt," Cody said affectionately, reaching down to scratch behind Duke's ears. The dog's tail thumped against the porch floor in appreciation.

They sat in easy silence for several minutes, Cody finishing his pizza while Mitch continued the gentle rocking motion that had always calmed him, even as a child. The first stars appeared overhead, pin-pricks of silver against the deepening blue.

In a lull between cricket songs, Cody stretched, looking out at the yard. "Had a good talk with Earl today," he said casually. "He wants me to start handling the ordering for the power tools section. Says if I'm gonna be a manager, I need to know the inventory like the back of my hand."

Mitch stopped swinging. He turned slowly to Cody, a grin spreading across his face. "Manager? Earl offered you the full-time manager job? When did all this happen, and why am I just hearing about it?"

Pride swelled in his chest, warm and expansive. His little brother—the wild kid who'd given him more gray hairs than he could count, was now talking about managing a business. The thought was unexpectedly moving.

Cody shrugged, attempting nonchalance, but his eyes held a new steadiness. "It's not official yet, but Earl's planning to step back a bit next year, focus more on the specialty orders, and leave the day-to-day to me." He took a long drink of his tea. "Figured I'd wait to tell you until it was a done deal, but... yeah. He thinks I've got what it takes."

"Cody, that's... that's fantastic!" Mitch said, the words inadequate for the pride he felt. "Seriously. You'll knock it out of the park. You've got a good head for it, and people like you. They trust you."

"Yeah, well, it's a lot to learn," Cody admitted. "But it feels... good, you know? Like I'm actually building something here. Earl's a good boss, even if he hums off-key while he's doing inventory." He set his empty plate on top of the pizza box. "Honestly, a year ago, I wouldn't have thought I was capable of it. But working there, figuring things out... it's been better than I expected."

"You've always been capable," Mitch said firmly. "You just needed to find the right fit."

"Maybe." Cody wiped his hands on a napkin. "Or maybe I just needed to grow up enough to appreciate what was right in front of me all along." He watched Mitch, who had resumed a slow, thoughtful swing, his gaze fixed on the darkening horizon. "So, that's my excitement for the week. What about the Sheriff of Laurel Ridge? You've been quieter than Duke after a five-mile run. Something on that big, responsible mind of yours besides keeping the peace? And don't tell me it's just budget reports."

His tone was light, teasing, but his eyes were observant.

Mitch wasn't used to this—being the one with the personal dilemma. It was usually him guiding Cody or Tessa, offering advice or direction. A flicker of his default privacy rose, then ebbed. This was different. This was Beth.

He took a slow sip of tea. "Just... thinking. About Beth, mostly."

Cody leaned forward, elbows on his knees, all humor gone. "Yeah, I kinda figured. Saw you two at VBS. And Tessa hasn't stopped talking about how good you guys are together since that Sunday lunch." He paused, studying Mitch's face in the fading light. "You look... good, Mitch. When you're with her. You look like life is showing you it's worth living. You look happy. I've never seen you like this... ever."

The admission felt momentous, like stepping off a known path into uncharted territory. "Happy, yeah. That's a good word for it." Mitch looked directly at Cody, the evening's last light catching the sincerity in his eyes. "Cody... I think I'm in love with her."

A wave of certainty washed over him. No doubts, no second-guessing. Just a profound, quiet knowing.

Cody was quiet for a long moment, taking it in. Then, a slow whistle. "Wow. Love. That's... not a word you throw around, Mitch." He leaned back in his chair. "Okay. Tell me. What is it about her?"

"It's... everything. It's not one thing." Mitch struggled to articulate the depth of it. "When I'm with her, the noise in my head stops. All the responsibilities, the worries... they just fade. I can just be me."

The crickets chirped steadily in the growing darkness, filling the spaces between his words. Duke shifted positions, curling closer to Mitch's feet as if sensing the importance of the conversation.

"She's got this strength, you know?" Mitch continued, the words coming more easily now. "After everything with her ex, she rebuilt her life, her business. I admire that more than I can say. But there's this incredible softness to her too, this kindness that just... shines."

He rotated his glass slowly, watching the ice melt into the amber liquid. "She listens. Really listens. And she sees me. Not Sheriff Baker, duty-bound and serious. She sees the guy underneath all that. And she still... seems to like him. We laugh. About stupid things. I'd forgotten what that felt like."

Cody nodded, his expression serious. "That's rare. Finding some-one who gets the real you."

"And she's honest," Mitch added. "Today at breakfast, she told me about Matt, about how he broke her trust. It wasn't easy for her. But hearing it... it didn't scare me off. It made me want to be the kind of man who never makes her feel that way again."

He looked out at the first stars pricking the dark velvet sky. "I just know, Cody. It's like a compass in my chest finally pointing true north. It's her. She's the one."

A toad croaked from somewhere near the porch steps, a deep, throaty sound that punctuated the night. The smell of dew rising from the grass mingled with the lingering warmth of the summer day.

"She's taking it slow," Mitch said, "and she has every right to. 'One day at a time,' she said. And I'm good with that. More than good. If it takes the rest of my life for her to trust completely, then that's what I'll give."

A warmth spread through him at Cody's quiet attention, the lack of teasing, the genuine consideration in his brother's eyes. He'd really grown up in the years he'd been away.

Cody nodded slowly, absorbing it all. "Man, Mitch. That's... something else. She sounds incredible... like a woman I hope someday to find." He paused, then added, "And you deserve that, you know? After everything you did for me and Tessa, putting your life on hold. You deserve someone just for you. You deserve to set aside the parent role and be a man enjoying life."

The simple statement hit Mitch with unexpected force. How long had it been since anyone had considered what he deserved? What he needed? Since his father's death and his mother left them, he'd defined himself by what others required of him—responsibility, steadiness, sacrifice. The idea that he might deserve happiness for himself alone was almost foreign.

"Coming back here," Cody continued, "I thought I knew what I wanted, or what I should want. But it turns out, the best things, the real things... they don't always fit a plan. Like this manager thing with Earl. Never saw it coming. But it feels right." He leaned forward again. "Maybe it's the same with Beth. It just... is. And you follow it."

He gestured with his empty glass. "You've always been the one looking out, making the tough calls. Maybe it's okay to just... let this be good. Don't try to sheriff your way through it, just... feel it."

A genuine smile touched Mitch's lips. "Thanks, little brother. That's... some pretty good advice. When did you get so perceptive?"

"Hey, I learned from the best." Cody grinned. "And I've had a lot of time to observe people making questionable life choices—mostly my own." His expression softened. "But seriously, Mitch. I'm happy for you. Really."

They lapsed into a comfortable quiet again, the kind only shared history can forge. Duke let out a soft snore.

Mitch took a final sip of his now-cool tea, feeling a sense of peace he hadn't known in years. He felt grounded, sure. The anxiety that had characterized so much of his adult life—the constant vigilance, the weight of responsibility—felt lighter somehow, as if sharing it with Cody had redistributed the load.

Cody got up and stretched, collecting the empty glasses and balancing them on the pizza box. "Love you brother."

"Love you too."

As the screen door swung shut behind Cody, Mitch remained on the porch, a deep sense of gratitude filling him.

Just be Mitch. The thought settled, comfortable and right. He pictured Beth's smile, the way her eyes lit up when she laughed. Tomorrow. A quiet anticipation, unburdened by his usual caution, took root.

He gazed up at the night sky, now fully awash with stars. The Milky Way stretched across the blackness, a reminder of how vast the universe was, yet how intimately connected each small part remained. A verse from Sunday's scripture reading came to mind: "For I know the plans I have for you, declares the Lord, plans to prosper you and not to harm you, plans to give you hope and a future."

For years, he'd interpreted that verse as reassurance for others—those he counseled through difficult times, those seeking guidance. Tonight, for perhaps the first time, he allowed himself to receive it personally. To believe that his own future might hold more than duty and responsibility. That it might include joy. Partnership. Love.

Yeah, he thought. *This is good.*

Chapter 18

Beth caught Mitch stealing a glance at her as he turned onto River Road, his profile strong against the backdrop of leafy trees and blue sky.

"You sure you don't mind heading to the town park?" he asked, one hand steady on the wheel, the other resting casually on the console between them. "I know it gets crowded on Sundays."

Beth shifted the deli bag on her lap, the paper crinkling beneath her fingers. The enticing aroma of fresh bread and herbs filled the cab of the truck.

"Not at all," she replied, adjusting her sunglasses against the bright afternoon. "It's one of my favorite places."

The easy rhythm of their conversation made her smile. Just yesterday morning, Mitch's words had nearly overwhelmed her: *I'm falling for you, Beth. Hard.*

Now, here they were, driving toward their second "official" date with a picnic lunch after church. Not friends having lunch—a date. The thought sent a flutter of anticipation through her chest.

She studied him as he drove—the way his fingers tapped lightly against the steering wheel when they stopped at a light, the subtle crow's feet at the corners of his eyes that deepened when he smiled, the confident ease with which he navigated the familiar roads of Laurel Ridge. This was a man who had slowly, steadily worked his way into her heart.

"Weather couldn't be more perfect," Mitch commented, rolling down his window slightly. The breeze carried the scent of freshly cut grass and sun-warmed pavement. "Not too hot for July."

"It's beautiful," Beth agreed. "Makes me think of those perfect summer days when I was a kid—the kind that seemed to stretch forever."

Mitch chuckled, the sound warm and genuine. "I know exactly what you mean. Remember how summer vacation felt endless in June, but was suddenly almost over by August?"

"Yes!" Beth laughed. "Now I blink and half the year is gone."

As they approached the park entrance, the green expanse opened before them—families spread across picnic tables, children racing between playground equipment, teenagers tossing a football on the open field. The creek that bordered the eastern edge of the park glittered in the sunlight, a ribbon of silver winding through the landscape.

Mitch drove slowly past the main parking area, which was nearly full, and headed toward a smaller lot closer to the creek. "I know a good spot," he explained, "if you don't mind a short walk."

"Not at all," Beth replied as he parked.

She waited as Mitch reached behind the seat of his truck and pulled out a patchwork quilt, worn soft with age and use. The gesture struck her—he'd planned ahead.

"My grandmother made this," he explained, almost sheepishly. "It's seen better days, but I thought it would be perfect for a picnic."

They walked side by side along a narrow path that followed the creek, moving away from the more populated areas of the park. The sounds of splashing water against rocks and rustling leaves gradually replaced the laughter and chatter of the main grounds. Beth breathed deeply, savoring the earthy richness of the creek bank mixed with the sweetness of late-blooming honeysuckle.

Mitch stopped at a small clearing shaded by mature oak trees. The spot offered a perfect view of the creek, which widened slightly here, creating a natural pool where the water slowed and deepened before continuing its journey.

He shook out the quilt and laid it on a level patch of grass. The breeze caught one corner, and Beth stepped forward to help, their hands briefly meeting as they secured the corners. She felt the calluses on his fingertips brush against her skin—a workingman's hands, strong yet surprisingly gentle.

"This is perfect," Beth said, settling onto the quilt and unpacking their lunch. She arranged the sandwiches, chips, and drinks between them. "How did you know about this spot?"

Mitch lowered himself beside her, leaning back on one hand. "Used to fish here as a kid. Dad would bring me and Cody when we were little. Later, I'd come alone when I needed to think." He gazed at the water. "Something about moving water always helps clear my head."

Beth handed him his sandwich—turkey and provolone on sourdough—and unwrapped her own chicken salad on wheat. "I can see why. It's peaceful here."

For a few minutes, they ate in easy companionship, the background symphony of birds, rustling leaves, and flowing water filling the silence. A blue jay called sharply from a nearby branch, and somewhere downstream, a fish jumped with a subtle splash.

Beth took a sip of her lemonade, the tart sweetness refreshing against the warmth of the day. "Pastor Andrew's sermon really spoke to me today."

Mitch nodded, setting aside his sandwich wrapper. "Romans 15:4. 'For everything that was written in the past was written to teach us, so that through the endurance taught in the Scriptures and the encouragement they provide, we might have hope.'" He smiled at her surprised expression. "I paid attention."

"Wow... your memory of bible verses is impressive. The sermon today... it just... resonated," Beth continued, drawing her knees up and wrapping her arms around them. "The idea that our struggles—our endurance—can actually lead to hope. That's not how we usually think about difficult times."

"How do you see it applying to your life?" Mitch asked, his question gentle but direct.

Beth considered, watching the play of sunlight through leaves, creating shifting patterns on the quilt between them. "I think... after Matt, I focused so much on enduring, on just getting through each day, rebuilding my life. I didn't see how those painful experiences were actually preparing me for something better." She met his gaze. "Teaching me what I truly needed and wanted."

"For me," Mitch offered, "it makes me think about raising Tessa and Cody. Those years were hard—a lot of responsibility, and a lot of sacrifice. But they taught me things I couldn't have learned any other way." He picked up a small stone, turning it over in his fingers. "And now, looking back, I can see God's hand in it all. The endurance shaped me, but I didn't always see the hope part until... recently."

"It's strange, isn't it?" she mused. "How the worst moments of our lives can somehow prepare us for the best ones?"

Mitch nodded, understanding in his eyes. "That's faith, I think. Trusting that even the painful parts have purpose."

Beth stood up, gathering their trash. "I'll be right back," she said, walking toward a nearby bin.

As she disposed of their lunch remnants, she paused, taking in the surrounding park. In the distance, a father pushed his daughter on a swing, her delighted squeals carrying across the grass. A couple walked hand-in-hand along the main path, their gray heads close together in conversation. An elderly man sat on a bench, tossing bread to eager ducks.

Life, in all its ordinary glory. The simple joys she'd almost convinced herself she didn't deserve.

Returning to the quilt, Beth found Mitch watching her, a gentle expression warming his features. She settled beside him again.

"Penny for your thoughts," Mitch said.

"Just enjoying the day," Beth replied. "Sometimes happiness sneaks up on you, doesn't it? In the quietest moments."

Mitch nodded, then lay back on the quilt, hands clasped behind his head as he gazed up at the canopy of leaves and patches of blue sky above them.

"Beth?" Mitch's voice was thoughtful.

"Hmm?" She turned to look at him.

"What do you dream about?" He turned to face her, his expression earnest. "I mean... deep down. Where do you see yourself ten, twenty years from now? What do you want out of life?"

The question caught her off guard—not because it was intrusive, but because it had been so long since anyone had asked about her dreams. Matt had always redirected conversations to his ambitions and his own needs.

"Well, I hope Mountain Chic is still thriving," she began cautiously. "And maybe the children's store will have expanded by then—"

"No, Beth." Mitch's interruption was gentle. He reached for her hand, his fingers intertwining with hers. "Set work aside for a minute. What do you want out of life? What are your heart's desires?"

The tenderness in his question nearly undid her. Beth lay back on the quilt beside him, their joined hands resting between them, and stared up at the brilliant blue sky where white clouds drifted like islands in an azure sea.

"I want..." she began, then paused, searching for words she hadn't allowed herself to voice in so long. "I want to stop being afraid. Afraid of making mistakes, afraid of trusting, and afraid of getting hurt again. I want to embrace joy, even the small, everyday joys, without waiting for the other shoe to drop."

Mitch's thumb traced small circles on the back of her hand, encouraging her to continue.

"And yes, it might sound cliché, but I dream of a family." The admission felt raw, exposing a longing she'd buried. "A home filled with love and laughter... children running through the yard."

She turned her head slightly to look at him, finding his eyes on her, patient and attentive.

"I want that house with the white picket fence, not for the fence itself, but for what it represents—a haven, a place where people feel welcome and loved. Sunday dinners with family and friends spilling out onto the porch." Beth smiled, the image vivid in her mind. "My grandmother used to host those kinds of dinners. The noise, the chaos, the togetherness... I miss that."

"It sounds wonderful," Mitch said.

"And I want it all here, in Laurel Ridge," Beth continued, her voice growing stronger. "This is my home, my roots. I tried living elsewhere once, during college, but it didn't feel right. This town, these mountains—they're part of who I am."

She took a deep breath, gathering courage. "I hope to grow old with someone by my side, a true partner. Rocking grand babies on that porch someday." She met his gaze directly, allowing her vulnerability to show. "Someone who sees me—really sees me—and chooses to stay, anyway."

Her dreams, spoken aloud, made her feel both lighter for having shared them and terrified of having exposed so much of herself.

Mitch's fingers tightened around hers, his expression solemn yet tender. A beat of silence passed, filled only by the gentle gurgle of the creek and the distant call of a cardinal.

"What about you, Mitch?" Beth asked, turning the question back to him. "What do you dream about?"

He exhaled slowly, his gaze returning to the sky above them. "Honestly, until recently, I hadn't let myself think much beyond ensuring Tessa and Cody were okay and keeping Laurel Ridge safe. My dreams were mostly for them."

"And now?" Beth prompted gently.

"Now..." A small smile played at the corners of his mouth. "Now I want more for myself. I want to actually live on my days off from work, not just catch up on paperwork. I want to travel a little, explore, maybe even learn something new just for the fun of it."

He shifted onto his side, facing her fully. "I want a partner, someone to share the quiet evenings with, not just the crises. Someone to laugh with over nothing, to build a life with, side-by-side."

Beth felt her heart quicken at the intensity of his gaze.

"And family..." Mitch continued, his voice dropping slightly. "The thought of having children of my own wasn't really on my radar before. But helping with VBS this year, seeing those kids light up, hearing their laughter... it's got me thinking about a home filled with that kind of joy."

The honesty in his admission touched Beth deeply. She could see what it cost him to voice these desires, to acknowledge his own needs after years of putting others first.

"That sounds like a beautiful dream," she whispered.

Mitch lifted their joined hands, pressing a tender kiss to her knuckles. The gesture, simple yet profound, sent warmth cascading through her.

She sat up suddenly, her heart pounding. Mitch followed, concern crossing his features.

"Beth? What's wrong?"

She turned to face him fully, taking in the warmth of his brown eyes, the strength in his features, the genuine care that radiated from him. This wasn't Matt. This wasn't the same risk. This was Mitch—steady, honest, kind Mitch.

"Nothing. Everything is perfect."

Before doubt could claim her courage, Beth leaned forward and pressed her lips to his. The kiss was gentle yet deliberate, a physical manifestation of the trust she was choosing to place in him, in them. His initial surprise gave way immediately as he responded, one hand coming up to cup her cheek with exquisite tenderness.

The world narrowed to this moment—the warmth of his touch, the softness of his lips against hers, the mingled scents of creek water and summer grass and Mitch's subtle cologne. She felt sixteen and ancient all at once, as if she were experiencing her first kiss and coming home after a long journey in the same heartbeat.

When they parted, Mitch's smile matched her own—wondering, joyful, and a little shy. His thumb brushed gently across her cheekbone.

"That was…" he began.

"Just the beginning," Beth finished, certainty blooming in her chest like the wildflowers dotting the creek bank—vibrant, unexpected, and perfectly, naturally right.

Chapter 19

Beth squinted at her laptop screen, massaging her temples as she scrutinized the latest vendor pricing. The spreadsheet blurred before her eyes, numbers swimming together after an hour of concentrated work. She'd skipped breakfast in her rush to get to the boutique this morning, and now her stomach protested with a quiet but persistent rumble.

Just as she contemplated closing her laptop for a much-needed break, movement in her peripheral vision caught her attention. Mitch stood in her open office doorway, leaning casually against the frame, his sheriff's badge glinting on his uniform. He held up a paper bag from Martha's Diner, a slight smile playing at the corners of his mouth.

"Working hard, or hardly working?" he asked, his eyes crinkling with warmth.

Beth's face broke into a surprised smile, her spreadsheet instantly forgotten. "Mitch! What are you doing here?"

"Thought you might be hungry." He lifted the bag slightly. "Care to join me for lunch? Maybe sit in the town square?"

A rush of warmth flooded through her at the thoughtful gesture. The contrast struck her briefly—Matt would never have interrupted his workday to bring her lunch—but she quickly pushed the thought aside, refusing to let the old shadows dim this moment.

"You read my mind," she said, closing her laptop. "I was just thinking about food." She stood, smoothing her navy dress. "I'd love to."

Three days had passed since their picnic by the creek, since that kiss that had changed everything between them. Each day since had brought text messages, phone conversations, and now this surprise visit.

"How did you know I'd be free?" she asked, stepping around her desk.

"I didn't." His admission came with a small shrug. "Just took a chance. Figured the worst that could happen was I'd have to eat Martha's pepperoni rolls all by myself."

"That would have been a tragedy, and one I'm happy to help you avoid," Beth teased, falling into step beside him.

As they walked through the boutique's main floor, Mitch reached for her hand, his fingers intertwining with hers in a gesture that felt both new and somehow familiar. Beth felt a little thrill at the contact, at the simple rightness of it.

Alisha looked up from arranging a display, her eyebrows raising at their joined hands, before her expression settled into a knowing smile. Pearl, dusting nearby shelves, beamed like she'd personally orchestrated their meeting.

"Ladies, I'm stepping out for lunch," Beth announced, feeling a slight blush warm her cheeks. "Not sure when I'll be back."

"Oh, you go right ahead, honey!" Pearl waved them off with enthusiasm. "Enjoy that sunshine and good company."

"Have fun, you two," Alisha added. "Don't worry about a thing here."

Mitch held the door for Beth, the July sun warm against their skin as they crossed main street. The town bustled with its usual midweek activity, tourists and locals wandering between shops. Across the street in the town square, multiple people sat enjoying their lunch breaks and children ran around the central gazebo. The colorful flower baskets hanging from lampposts swayed gently in the summer breeze.

"Where would you like to sit?" Mitch asked, gesturing toward the park benches scattered throughout the square.

Beth glanced around, then her eyes lit up with sudden inspiration. "You know... how about the swinging bridge?"

Mitch's smile widened. "Perfect."

They walked along the edge of the town square, following the path that connected to the riverside walkway. The New River gleamed ahead, sunlight dancing across its surface like scattered diamonds. The wooden swinging bridge—a historic landmark connecting the town square area to multiple hiking trails on the opposite bank—stretched before them.

"I haven't been out here in a while," Beth admitted as they stepped onto the bridge, feeling the subtle give beneath their feet.

"Me neither," Mitch said.

They found a spot in the middle of the bridge, settling down to dangle their legs over the edge. The gentle sway created a pleasant rocking sensation, reminiscent of childhood swings. Beneath them, the river flowed steadily, its rushing sounds mingling with the distant chatter from the town square.

Mitch opened the paper bag, the aroma of pepperoni rolls wafting out and making Beth's mouth water. He passed her one, wrapped in wax paper, still warm to the touch, along with a small container of pasta salad and a bottle of water.

"Martha insisted I take these too," he said, pulling out two caramel brownies. "Said something about 'that girl needs more than just a pepperoni roll, she deserves a little something sweet.'"

"Martha's on a mission to fatten me up," Beth laughed, unwrapping her pepperoni roll. The first bite was heavenly—savory and rich, with Martha's secret blend of spices and cheese. "Oh, I needed this."

The bridge swayed gently as a couple with a stroller crossed, nodding in friendly greeting as they passed. A pair of mallards floated lazily beneath them, occasionally dipping underwater in search of food.

"How's your day been?" Beth asked, savoring another bite.

"Pretty quiet, thankfully." Mitch twisted the cap off his water bottle. "Mrs. Henderson called about a suspicious squirrel in her yard—third time this month."

"Let me guess... it was eating from her bird feeder again?"

"Worse. It was making faces at her through the window." Mitch's expression remained deadpan. "I tried explaining that squirrels don't actually make faces, but she insisted this one was plotting something."

Beth nearly choked on her pasta salad, laughter bubbling up. "And did you apprehend this criminal mastermind?"

"Sadly, the perpetrator had fled the scene before I arrived. But I assured Mrs. Henderson we'd keep an eye out for any squirrels exhibiting suspicious behavior."

Their laughter mingled with the rushing water beneath them. Beth felt a lightness she hadn't experienced in years—the simple joy of sharing ridiculous stories with someone who made her feel safe enough to laugh freely.

"Aside from squirrel surveillance, it's been a slow day," Mitch continued. "Gave me more time to think about... other things." His eyes met hers with gentle intensity.

Beth felt her cheeks warm again. "Oh? What kinds of things?"

"This," he said simply, gesturing between them. "Us. How much I've been looking forward to seeing you again."

"Me too."

Beth took a deep breath, suddenly feeling the excitement of her news pressing against her chest, demanding to be shared. "Well, my morning was quiet in one way, but pretty monumental in another..." She paused, a mixture of excitement and nervousness bubbling up. "I did it, Mitch. I signed the lease on the Cedar Street space this morning. The children's store is officially happening!"

The words rushed out in a torrent of excitement. Saying it aloud made it real in a way that even signing the papers hadn't. This was her dream—the one she'd put aside during her marriage, the one she'd slowly reclaimed after Matt left. And now it was becoming reality.

Mitch's face broke into a wide, proud grin. His hand found hers, squeezing gently. "Beth, that's incredible! Fantastic news!" His voice carried genuine enthusiasm. "I knew you could do it."

Pride swelled in her chest at his reaction. There was no hint of competition, no subtle diminishing of her achievement—just pure, unfiltered support.

"This is huge!" Mitch continued, enthusiasm radiating from him. "We have to celebrate. This isn't just 'signing a lease'; it's you making your dream a reality."

"Oh, well, it's just the first step, really. There's so much to do—renovations, ordering inventory, hiring staff—"

"Nope." Mitch cut her off gently but firmly, covering her hand with his. "Every major step deserves to be celebrated. You've worked hard for this, Beth."

The sincerity in his voice touched her. He was right. This was a moment worth celebrating, worth acknowledging as the achievement it was.

"You're right."

They finished their lunch; the bridge swaying gently beneath them. A group of teenagers passed, laughing and jostling each other. Below, a fisherman had set up on the riverbank, his line arcing gracefully over the water.

Mitch looked thoughtful for a moment, his expression shifting as if an idea were taking shape. "Can you get away from the store around four o'clock this evening?"

Beth raised her eyebrows, intrigued by the sudden question. "I think I can manage that... Why? What are you scheming, Sheriff Baker?"

Mitch leaned in slightly, his voice dropping to a near-whisper, though no one was close enough to overhear. "Do you trust me?"

Beth looked into his eyes—steady, honest, warm—and found her answer without hesitation.

"Yes, Mitch. I do trust you."

A slow, pleased smile spread across his face, reaching all the way to his eyes. "Good." He squeezed her hand. "Then I'll pick you up from the boutique at four. And wear something... well, just be ready for a nice evening."

"That's very mysterious," she teased, a flutter of anticipation stirring in her chest.

"A little mystery is good for the soul," he replied with a small smile.

They gathered their lunch containers, Mitch tucking everything back into the paper bag to dispose of properly. As they stood to leave, Beth felt the bridge sway more pronouncedly with their movement, a physical reminder of the shifting ground beneath her feet these past few days.

"I should get back to the station," Mitch said as they reached the town square side of the bridge. "Reed's covering for me, but I don't want to push my luck."

"And I should check on Pearl and Alisha," Beth agreed. "Make sure they haven't rearranged my entire store in my absence."

They walked back toward Main Street, their hands finding each other again naturally.

Outside Mountain Chic, they paused. Beth was acutely aware of the storefront windows and the potential audience inside, but found she didn't care as much as she might have once.

"Thank you for lunch," she said. "It was a wonderful surprise."

"My pleasure." Mitch's eyes crinkled at the corners. "I'll see you at four?"

"I'll be ready," she promised.

Mitch hesitated a moment, then leaned down and pressed a quick, gentle kiss to her cheek. "Congratulations again on the lease, Beth. It's a big deal, and I'm proud of you."

The simple sincerity of his words warmed her more than the summer sun. "Thank you for saying that."

As Mitch headed back toward the sheriff's department, Beth stood outside her boutique, watching him go with a smile she couldn't suppress. Through the window, she caught Pearl's not-so-subtle thumbs-up and Alisha's knowing grin.

With a small laugh, Beth pushed open the door, her heart feeling light.

Chapter 20

The afternoon flew by in a whirlwind of customer interactions and paperwork. Beth glanced at the clock with increasing frequency as four o'clock approached. At three-fifteen, she retreated to her office, refreshing her makeup and letting her hair down from its workday ponytail.

"You know, I could handle the store if you wanted to leave a little early," Alisha suggested, appearing in the doorway. Her eyes took in Beth's refreshed appearance with approval. "You know... go home and get ready for your date... Or, better yet... how about that burgundy dress we just got in?"

"The Burgundy dress?" Beth asked, looking down at what she wore.

"You're going somewhere special with a certain tall, handsome law enforcement officer? So yes, the burgundy dress." Alisha grinned.

"I think I will. Take one of the size ten's out of inventory."

"I can do that and shoes?"

"Take a pair of the new heels that came in yesterday out of inventory too…size eight and a half."

"I'm on it. I'll grab the dress and the heels and be right back," Alisha confirmed cheerfully, before disappearing around the corner.

Beth sat down in the chair behind her desk and smiled. Life was turning out to be pretty darn good. She thought to herself as tears started to form in her eyes.

"Beth… no… no crying. This is good. You should be happy," Alisha said as she entered the office. The dress hung over her arm and a shoebox in one hand.

Beth looked at Alisha, smiled and fanned her face. "These are happy tears."

"Good…. You scared me for a minute. Now get up and change. Fix your makeup and go celebrate," Alisha said as she closed the office door.

Beth rushed, kicking off her shoes and changing into the gorgeous new sundress. She gave her makeup a quick touch up and a final glance in the mirror that hung on the back of her office door. The burgundy dress fit her body perfectly. Around her neck hung a delicate silver necklace, her hair fell in loose natural waves, and the black sling back heels looked perfect. She took a deep breath and smiled.

When she opened her office door, Mitch stood there in dark gray slacks and a blue button-down shirt, the color bringing out the rich brown of his eyes. She noted he'd taken extra care with his appearance—his hair neatly combed, a subtle cologne detectable in the air between them.

For a moment, they simply looked at each other, a shared appreciation passing between them.

"You look beautiful," Mitch said finally, his voice warm with sincerity.

Beth felt a slight flush rise to her cheeks. "You clean up pretty well yourself, Sheriff."

"Not 'Sheriff' tonight," he corrected gently. "Just Mitch."

She smiled, "So, just Mitch, are you going to tell me where we're going?" she asked as he guided her through the store and out to his truck with a light hand at the small of her back.

"That would ruin the surprise." He opened the passenger door for her. "But I promise its nothing too elaborate. Just something I thought you might enjoy."

The summer evening was perfect—warm but not oppressive. As they drove through town, Beth noticed they were heading toward the outskirts, following the river road that wound its way along the New River.

"How are you feeling about the children's store?" Mitch asked, his eyes on the road ahead. "Now that it's official."

Beth considered the question. "Excited. Terrified. Proud." She smiled, watching the scenery pass outside her window. "It's something I've wanted for so long, but kept putting off. This new store—it feels like I'm finally building something just for me because I want to, not because I'm trying to prove anything."

Mitch nodded, understanding in his expression. "That's a good place to create from."

The road curved alongside the river; the water catching the late afternoon sunlight in rippling patterns. After a few more miles, Mitch turned onto a smaller road that Beth recognized as leading to one of the local wineries.

"River Bend Vineyard?" she asked, spotting the sign ahead.

Mitch glanced over with a smile. "They're hosting a small event tonight that I thought you might enjoy."

As they approached, Beth saw that the vineyard's terrace had been transformed. String lights hung between wooden posts, creating a canopy of soft illumination. Small tables covered in white cloths were arranged to face a small stage area where musicians were setting up. A banner read "Summer Music Series—Jazz Night."

"I remembered you mentioning how much you loved jazz when we were talking during VBS setup," Mitch explained as he parked. "And I knew River Bend started these Thursday night concerts recently..."

Beth felt a surge of emotion at the thoughtfulness of his surprise. "You remembered that? I barely mentioned it."

"I pay attention to the things you say," he replied simply as he parked the truck.

The vineyard was already filling with people—a mixture of tourists and locals, settling at tables with glasses of wine and small plates of food.

"Mr. Baker," a server, greeted them with a warm smile as they approached. "Your table is ready, as requested."

"You made reservations?" Beth asked once they were seated.

"I called this afternoon, right after lunch," Mitch admitted. "They were booked, but when I mentioned it was to celebrate your new business venture, the owner said he would add another table."

"The perks of being the sheriff everyone loves," Beth teased.

"More like the perks of small-town connections. Martha's niece manages events here."

The server returned with two glasses of wine—a light rosé that glowed amber-pink in the early evening light—and a small cheese board with local honey, fruits, and artisanal crackers.

"A toast," Mitch said, raising his glass. "To you, businesswoman extraordinaire, making dreams reality one lease at a time."

Beth laughed, clinking her glass against his. "That's quite a title."

"You've earned it."

As the musicians began to play—a smooth, melodic jazz that filled the warm evening air—Beth found herself relaxing completely. The sun cast a golden light over the vineyard, illuminating the rows of grapevines that stretched toward the horizon. The music washed over them, sometimes lively and bright, other times rich and soulful.

They talked about plans for the children's store, about a hiking trail Mitch had discovered recently, about favorite books and childhood memories. The ease between them felt precious and rare, a connection that had grown steadily despite all her initial caution.

During a particularly beautiful saxophone solo, Beth found herself watching Mitch as he gazed at the musicians, genuinely absorbed in the performance. The strong line of his jaw, the thoughtful set of his mouth, the way his eyes reflected the string lights overhead—all of it struck her with sudden clarity.

I'm falling in love with him, she realized. The thought should have terrified her, but instead, it settled into her heart with a quiet certainty that felt like coming home.

As if sensing her gaze, Mitch turned to her, his expression softening. "What are you thinking about?" he asked.

"Just... how happy I am right now," she answered truthfully. "How right this feels."

He reached across the table, taking her hand in his. "It does, doesn't it?"

The music swelled around them, rich and hopeful, a perfect soundtrack to the emotions building in her chest.

"Beth," Mitch began, his thumb tracing gentle patterns on her palm, "I want you to know—"

"Well, if it isn't Sheriff Baker!" a voice interrupted. They looked up to see Earl Smith and his wife approaching their table. "Thought that was you sitting over here. Evening, Beth."

"Earl, Margaret," Mitch greeted them, releasing Beth's hand with obvious reluctance. "Enjoying the music?"

"Margaret's idea," Earl explained. "Says I need more culture than fishing reports and hardware catalogs."

"It's our anniversary," Margaret added with an affectionate pat to her husband's arm. "Forty-two years today."

"Congratulations," Beth said sincerely. "That's wonderful."

"The secret is separate bathrooms and selective hearing," Earl stage-whispered, earning a gentle swat from his wife.

"Don't listen to him," Margaret said with a laugh. "The secret is finding someone who makes you better, then choosing them every single day." Her eyes, warm with decades of love, met her husband's. "Even the hard days."

"Especially the hard days," Earl agreed, his gruff exterior softening as he looked at his wife.

Beth felt their words wash over her, the simple truth of a love that had weathered life's storms and emerged stronger. She glanced at Mitch and found him watching her, his expression tender.

"Well, we won't keep you," Margaret said, sensing the moment between them. "Enjoy your evening, you two."

As the older couple moved away, Mitch's eyes remained on Beth.

The music slowed to a more intimate melody that had several couples moving to the small dance area near the stage. Beth watched them, swaying gently to the rhythm, until Mitch stood and extended his hand to her.

"Dance with me?"

She placed her hand in his, allowing him to lead her to the dance floor. His arm encircled her waist with gentle pressure, drawing her close as they began to move in time with the music. Beth's hand rested on his shoulder, feeling the solid strength beneath her palm.

"I have a confession," Mitch said softly, his breath warm against her hair. "I'm not much of a dancer."

"You're doing just fine," she assured him, following his lead as they swayed together.

The evening air had cooled slightly, carrying the mingled scents of wine, earth, and the river beyond. Above them, the sun was starting to descend behind the mountains in the deepening blue of the sky, and the string lights created a cocoon of golden illumination around the terrace.

"What were you going to say earlier?" Beth asked after a moment. "Before Earl and Margaret came over."

Mitch's steps slowed slightly. His eyes, warm and serious, met hers. "I was going to say that being with you these past several days has been the happiest I've felt since I was a child." His voice lowered. "And that I'm falling in love with you, Beth. I have been since that first day at your boutique."

The words should have startled her, should have triggered all her old fears and defenses. Instead, they resonated with her own realization from moments earlier, fitting perfectly into the space in her heart that had been waiting for them.

"Mitch," she breathed, her voice catching slightly. "I—"

"You don't have to say anything," he assured her quickly. "I know it's soon. I know you're still healing, still finding your way forward. I just... wanted you to know where I stand. How I feel."

Beth stopped dancing, her hands moving to frame his face, thumbs brushing lightly against his cheekbones. The music continued around them, but they stood still, caught in a moment that felt suspended in time.

"I'm falling in love with you too," she said softly, the words carrying all the weight of her journey—the pain, the healing, the tentative hope that had blossomed into something stronger. "And it terrifies me and thrills me all at once."

His expression transformed, wonder and joy mingling in his eyes. "Beth..."

She rose on her tiptoes, closing the distance between them with a kiss that conveyed everything words couldn't capture—her trust, her hope, and her deepening feelings. His arms tightened around her waist, drawing her closer as he returned the kiss with equal tenderness.

When they parted, the music had shifted to a more upbeat tempo, but they remained in their own rhythm, foreheads touching, sharing the same breath.

"Thank you for today," Beth whispered. "For lunch on the bridge, for this perfect evening. For celebrating with me."

"This is just the beginning," Mitch promised, his voice low and certain. "Of celebrations, of us... of everything."

As the sun dipped below the horizon, painting the sky in vivid streaks of pink and gold, Beth believed him. It was the beginning of something even more beautiful. A future she was ready to embrace, with a man who had proven worthy of her trust.

One day at a time had become day after wonderful day. And tonight, that was more than enough.

Chapter 21

Beth's footsteps echoed on the worn linoleum floor of the Laurel Ridge Sheriff's Department, a spring in her step matching the lightness in her heart. The brown paper bag from Martha's Diner swung gently in her hand, as the aroma of freshly baked bread and Martha's special roast beef wafted upward. She'd impulsively decided to surprise Mitch for lunch.

Days had passed since their evening at River Bend Vineyard, days of lingering smiles and private joy whenever she remembered Mitch's words: I'm falling in love with you, Beth. She still felt the pleasant shiver those words had sent through her, matching her own confession perfectly. The memory of their dances beneath the string lights, his arms steady around her waist, had carried her through the week on a cloud of newfound certainty.

"Morning, Cheryl," Beth greeted the dispatcher who sat at the front desk, typing away at her computer.

Cheryl looked up with a smile of recognition. "Well, hello there, Ms. Rutledge! What brings you by?"

Beth lifted the bag slightly. "Thought I'd surprise the sheriff with lunch. Is he in?"

"Sure is. He's been holed up in his office all morning with paperwork." Cheryl winked. "He could use the distraction, if you ask me. Go on back—you know the way."

Beth nodded her thanks and headed down the hallway toward Mitch's office. Her heels clicked against the floor as she walked, anticipation building.

The door to his office stood partially open. Beth approached, a greeting ready on her lips, when the sound of Mitch's voice—strained in a way she'd never heard before—stopped her short.

"Yes, sir, I understand the scope."

Beth paused, not wanting to interrupt. Through the gap in the door, she could see Mitch's back as he stood behind his desk, one hand gripping the phone, the other pressed flat against a stack of papers.

"Charleston... yes."

The mention of the state capital caught Beth's attention. Charleston was nearly two hours away.

"A rural crimes task force... FBI."

Beth froze, the bag in her hand suddenly forgotten. FBI? The three letters hung in the air, laden with implications she couldn't immediately process.

"That's... quite an honor, sir." Mitch's voice carried an undercurrent of shock, though he maintained his professional tone.

Beth's stomach tightened as she listened, rooted to the spot outside his door.

"Two weeks to consider... I appreciate that. Yes, sir. I will give it serious consideration."

The words echoed in her mind. Serious consideration. Her grip on the lunch bag tightened imperceptibly.

"Thank you again."

As Mitch replaced the phone in its cradle, Beth watched him run both hands through his hair, his shoulders rising and falling with a deep breath. He turned slightly, revealing his profile—his expression stunned, eyebrows drawn together in thought.

Beth knocked softly on the door.

Mitch turned fully, his eyes widening in surprise. "Beth." He managed a smile, though it didn't reach his eyes.

She stepped into the office, holding up the lunch bag as an explanation. "I thought I'd surprise you with lunch." She searched his face. "Mitch? Is everything alright? You look like you've seen a ghost."

He moved around his desk, gesturing for her to take a seat in one of the chairs. "I... uh... just had a rather unexpected call."

The hesitation in his voice, so unlike his usual steady confidence, sent a flicker of unease through her. She set the lunch bag on his desk and sank into the chair, her eyes never leaving his face.

"What kind of call?" she asked, though part of her already knew—had heard enough to piece together a scenario that made her heart beat faster with apprehension.

Mitch leaned against his desk, physically closer to her but somehow distant in his demeanor. "An interesting phone call. William Davis, the Assistant Director of the FBI's Criminal Division. They're... they're creating a new rural crimes task force to address issues across West Virginia, Kentucky, and Tennessee. Drug trafficking, equipment theft, agricultural crime—things that affect rural communities but often fall through jurisdictional cracks."

He paused, his eyes meeting hers briefly, before looking away. "They want me to head it up. Based in Charleston."

"Charleston," Beth repeated, the word falling like a stone between them.

"Yeah." Mitch shook his head slightly, as if still processing it himself. "It's a significant opportunity, a real honor. But... Charleston?"

Beth nodded mechanically, her mind racing. Charleston wasn't just a city two hours away—it was Matt's new home with his new woman. It was the urban center that had lured her ex-husband away with promises of bigger opportunities and a more exciting life. Now it beckoned to Mitch as well.

"Wow, Mitch. That's... a big deal. The FBI?" She kept her voice even and controlled, despite the alarm bells clanging in her head.

"I never expected anything like this," Mitch continued, pacing a few steps. "Davis cited my work on that cross-county equipment theft ring last year and the meth lab investigation. He said my understanding of rural dynamics is what they're looking for."

Beth watched him move, noting the energy in his steps—not excitement exactly, but something that looked unsettlingly like consideration. Her stomach churned.

"Is it... is it something you'd want, Mitch? Something you've ever thought about?" She kept her tone carefully neutral, though her fingers gripped the armrests of her chair.

Mitch stopped pacing and leaned back against his desk, eyes fixed on a point beyond her shoulder. "Honestly, Beth, I've never imagined working anywhere but here. My life is here. But, on a purely professional level, an offer like this... it's something. It's an honor to even be considered."

Each word felt like a tiny pin piercing the bubble of security she'd begun to build around their relationship. He was considering it. She could see it in the furrow of his brow, hear it in the way his voice lifted slightly when he mentioned the honor of being chosen.

"But that doesn't mean... I can't see myself leaving. Especially not now." His eyes met hers meaningfully, but something in his expression—a shadow of internal conflict—made his reassurance ring hollow in Beth's ears.

Especially not now. The phrase echoed. *What did that mean? Especially not now that we've found each other? Or especially not now that I've just declared my feelings, making this more complicated?*

Beth stood suddenly, needing physical distance as memories and fears crashed over her like waves. "Well, it certainly sounds like a significant opportunity. You should definitely take the time to think about it."

Confusion crossed Mitch's face. "Think about it? Beth, I just told you... So, what about lunch? That's why you're here, right?" He gestured toward the forgotten bag on his desk.

Beth glanced at it, the sight of it now almost painful. She'd come here feeling secure and spontaneous, wanting to share an ordinary moment in the extraordinary new reality of their relationship. Now that reality felt as fragile as the paper bag, liable to tear open at the slightest pressure.

"This news... it's a lot to take in." She forced a small, sad smile. "You clearly have a lot on your mind. You need space to process this without... without me in the picture, clouding your judgment."

Mitch stood straighter, his expression sharpening. "Clouding my judgment? Beth, you're not... I don't want the job." A note of hurt crept into his voice.

But Beth's defenses had risen fully now, protecting her from the pain she was sure would come.

"Mitch, please." She reached for her purse, needing the comfort of something to hold. "An offer like this doesn't come along every day. You owe it to yourself to consider it seriously."

He stepped toward her, his expression a mixture of frustration and bewilderment. "But I... we..." He seemed at a loss for words.

Beth couldn't bear to see that look—couldn't bear to watch him struggle between his feelings for her and this professional opportunity. It was too much. She needed to get out before her composure cracked completely.

"Take some time, Mitch. Really think this through." She manufactured a quick, brittle smile. "I should go... give you some space. Let you get back to... everything."

Before he could protest further, before he could see the tears beginning to gather in her eyes, Beth turned and walked swiftly from the office. Her heels echoed down the hallway, each click a counterpoint to the thoughts pounding in her head.

"Beth?" Cheryl called as she passed the front desk. "Everything okay, honey?"

"Fine," Beth managed, not slowing her pace. "Just remembered something urgent at the boutique."

The midday sun assaulted her eyes as she pushed through the department's front doors, the brightness seeming to mock her darkened mood.

Charleston.

The name taunted her with memories of Matt's betrayal, of being left behind while he pursued another woman and his ambitions. She'd rebuilt her life, her confidence, her heart—only to find herself right back where she started, facing the prospect of being secondary to someone's career goals.

Her phone vibrated in her purse. She pulled it out to see Mitch's name on the screen. She couldn't answer—not now, not when she was barely holding herself together. Beth switched it to silent and dropped it back into her purse.

When she reached the store, Beth realized she'd walked the entire way from the sheriff's department without conscious awareness of her surroundings. She paused outside, drawing a deep breath and composing her features before pushing open the door.

Pearl looked up from arranging a display of summer scarves. "How was lunch with our handsome sheriff?" Her smile faltered as she took in Beth's expression. "Honey? What happened?"

Beth shook her head, unable to form the words. The concern in Pearl's eyes nearly undid her carefully maintained facade.

"Beth?" Alisha emerged from the stockroom, carrying a box of new inventory. She set it down immediately upon seeing Beth's face. "What's wrong?"

"I... I can't..." Beth gestured vaguely toward her office. "I need a minute."

She retreated to the sanctuary of her small office, closing the door behind her with a quiet click. Only then did she allow her shoulders to slump, her breath coming in shaky gasps as she sank into her chair.

The irony wasn't lost on her. Just days ago, she'd stood in this same office preparing for an evening that had culminated in exchanging declarations of love. Now she sat here with those same words, feeling like ashes in her mouth.

Her phone vibrated, alerting her of an incoming text: Beth, please call me. I don't understand what just happened. We need to talk about this.

She set the phone face-down on her desk, unable to respond. What could she say? I'm terrified you'll choose your career over me? I'm afraid to compete with the FBI for your attention?

A soft knock at the door interrupted her spiraling thoughts.

"Beth?" Leslie's voice came through the wood. "Alisha called me. Can I come in?"

Beth wiped hastily at her eyes. "It's open."

Leslie slipped in, quietly closing the door behind her. One look at Beth's face, and she crossed the small office, perching on the edge of the desk.

"What happened?" she asked simply.

The floodgates opened. Beth told her everything—the surprise lunch, the overheard phone call, the offer in Charleston, Mitch's obvious internal conflict despite his reassurances.

"When he was on the phone, he said he'd give it 'serious consideration,'" Beth finished, her voice hollow. "I heard him say those exact words. And when I asked him about it, he admitted it was an honor to be considered."

Leslie listened without interruption, her expression thoughtful. When Beth fell silent, she reached for her friend's hand.

"First of all, breathe," she instructed gently. "Second, this doesn't sound anything like what happened with Matt."

"Doesn't it?" Beth withdrew her hand, standing to pace the small confines of her office. "An amazing career opportunity in Charleston? Telling me one thing while clearly thinking about another? How is that different?"

"Because Mitch isn't Matt," Leslie countered firmly. "From what you've just told me, Mitch was shocked by this offer—not actively pursuing it behind your back. And he immediately told you he couldn't see himself leaving, especially now that you two are—"

"Words," Beth interrupted, wrapping her arms around herself. "Matt said all the right words, too."

Leslie's expression softened with understanding. "Beth, honey, I know you're scared. After what Matt did to you, anyone would be. But Mitch has proven himself trustworthy in every way."

"I thought I knew Matt too," Beth whispered. "I was wrong then. How can I be certain I'm not wrong now?"

"Because you're not the same person you were then," Leslie reminded her. "You're stronger, wiser. And Mitch has shown his character in countless ways that have nothing to do with words. Actions, Beth. Look at his actions."

Beth sank back into her chair, conflicting emotions warring within her. Leslie was right—Mitch had consistently shown himself to be honorable, trustworthy, and genuine. Nothing in his behavior had ever given her reason to doubt him.

And yet...

"I need time," she said finally. "I told him to think about the offer, and I meant it. He should consider it fully, without any pressure from me." Her chin lifted slightly. "And I need to protect myself, Les. I can't go through heartbreak again."

Leslie studied her for a long moment. "That's fair. But promise me something?"

"What?"

"Don't make decisions based on fear. Pray about this, Beth. Ask for wisdom. Remember who you are now, not who you were when Matt hurt you. Really think about the phone call you overheard. Think about the conversation you just had with Mitch. Then think about how you responded."

Beth nodded, though the knot in her chest didn't loosen.

After Leslie left, Beth sat alone in her office, staring at the phone still lying face-down on her desk.

Her phone vibrated again. With trembling fingers, she turned it over: Beth I don't know what happened, but please don't shut me out. Whatever you're thinking, whatever you're afraid of, we can talk about it. I'm not going anywhere.

The words blurred as tears filled her eyes. I'm not going anywhere. How she wanted to believe that.

Chapter 22

Mitch stared at the open doorway. His office felt hollow with Beth's absence. The sound of her heels clicking down the hallway faded, leaving only the harsh buzz of fluorescent lights and the quiet hum of his desktop computer. The lunch bag from the diner sat abandoned on his desk, its brown paper creased where Beth's fingers had gripped it moments ago.

He picked up the bag, the warmth of freshly made food still radiating through the paper, then set it back down.

You need space to process this without... without me in the picture, clouding your judgment.

Her words replayed in his mind, each syllable striking like a physical blow. *Clouding his judgment?*

How had everything unraveled so quickly? One unexpected phone call, and suddenly the woman who'd kissed him with such certainty was pulling away.

Mitch sank into his chair, pulling his phone from his pocket.

The call went straight to Beth's voicemail.

He tried a text instead: Beth, please call me. I don't understand what just happened. We need to talk about this.

He set the phone down, his gaze falling on the notepad where he'd jotted details from Assistant Director Davis's call. The position sounded impressive on paper—heading a three-state rural crimes task force, addressing issues that affected communities like Laurel Ridge but often went overlooked due to jurisdictional complications. Professionally, it represented a recognition of everything he'd done in his career.

And yet, sitting alone in his office with the lingering scent of a lunch meant to be shared, the offer felt like nothing more than a destructive force he hadn't invited into his life.

Mitch rubbed his hand over his face as Reed entered his office.

"Everything okay, Sheriff?"

"Fine," Mitch replied automatically, straightening in his chair. "Just handling some unexpected news."

Reed hesitated. "Beth left in a hurry. Cheryl mentioned she seemed upset."

Mitch's jaw tightened.

"It's complicated," he said finally. "I need to sort some things out."

Reed nodded, understanding the dismissal. "Let me know if you need anything. I'm headed out on patrol."

Alone again, Mitch checked his phone. No response from Beth. He tried another text: Beth, I don't know what happened, but please don't shut me out. Whatever you're thinking, whatever you're afraid of, we can talk about it. I'm not going anywhere.

The words stared back at him from the screen. I'm not going anywhere. That's what he'd tried to tell her in person, but she hadn't seemed to hear him—or worse, hadn't believed him.

Mitch pushed back from his desk, unable to focus on work, and grabbed his keys. "Cheryl, I'm heading out for a bit," he called as he passed the front desk. "Call my cell if anything urgent comes up."

The midday heat hit him as he stepped outside, the July sun beating down on the parking lot.

Main Street was bustling with midday activity as Mitch drove through town. He passed Mountain Chic, slowing instinctively, but forced himself to continue. As much as every fiber of his being wanted to march in there and clear up whatever misunderstanding had occurred, he respected her enough to let her be for now.

The familiar route home passed in a blur of green fields and scattered farmhouses. Mitch's knuckles whitened as he gripped the steering wheel, replaying Beth's reaction in his mind.

It wasn't just the abruptness of her departure that troubled him—it was the look in her eyes. Behind the carefully controlled expression, he'd glimpsed naked fear. Not disappointment or anger, but genuine fear.

Charleston. She had repeated Charleston. Where Matt had gone. Where her ex-husband had abandoned her for another woman and a more exciting life.

The realization hit Mitch with startling clarity: her fear wasn't about him considering a job offer—it was about history repeating itself in the most painful way possible.

Unfairness burned in his chest. He'd told her outright that he couldn't see himself leaving Laurel Ridge, especially not now. He'd given her no reason to doubt him, had proven himself trustworthy at every turn. Just days ago, he'd told her he was falling in love with her, and she'd said the same. How could she not trust that, even for a moment?

But even as frustration swelled, understanding followed close behind. Beth's wounds ran deeper than he'd realized.

Gravel crunched beneath his tires as he pulled up to his farmhouse. Duke bounded from the porch to greet him, tail wagging wildly. Mitch scratched behind the dog's ears, grateful for the simple, unconditional welcome.

Inside, he found Cody at the kitchen table, laptop open before him, papers scattered around.

"Hey," Cody greeted, glancing up. "You're home early."

Mitch grunted in response, heading straight for the coffeemaker. He didn't particularly want coffee, but the routine of measuring grounds and filling the reservoir gave his hands something to do.

Cody watched him silently for a moment, then closed his laptop. "Okay, what's up? You look like someone kicked you in the shins."

"Nothing." Mitch leaned against the counter, arms crossed. "Just work stuff."

Cody raised an eyebrow. "Sure. You've got that same look you had when Mom left. Like someone pulled the rug out from under you."

The coffee maker gurgled to life, filling the kitchen with its rich aroma. Mitch stared at the dark liquid beginning to fill the carafe, debating how much to share.

"I got a job offer today," he said finally, the words feeling inadequate to describe the day's events.

"Okay?" Cody ventured cautiously.

"FBI. Rural crimes task force. Based in Charleston."

Cody whistled low. "Wow. That's major, Mitch."

"Yeah." Mitch grabbed two mugs from the cabinet, pouring coffee he didn't want. "Beth came in just as I was hanging up."

Understanding dawned on Cody's face. "Ah. And she didn't take it well."

"That's putting it mildly." Mitch set a mug in front of Cody. "I told her I couldn't see myself leaving Laurel Ridge, especially not now. But she..." His voice tightened. "She just shut down. Said I needed to think about it without her 'clouding' things."

Cody frowned. "Clouding things? What does that even mean?"

"Everything was perfect between us until today. Now, she's acting like I've already got one foot out the door."

Cody took a thoughtful sip of his coffee. "Did she say anything specific?"

"Just repeated the word Charleston, like it was significant." Mitch set his untouched mug aside. "Which I've thought about and that's where her ex moved with the woman he cheated on her with."

"Man, that's rough. Charleston's probably a loaded word for her."

"I just don't understand how she could think I'd..."

"Sounds like she's running scared, Mitch," Cody said quietly. "Not because of you, but because of what he did to her."

"She thinks I'm going to choose the job over her. Just like Matt chose his career and another woman over their marriage."

"Makes sense," Cody agreed. "Pain like that doesn't just disappear, even when you meet someone better. Maybe especially then."

Mitch looked at his brother with newfound respect.

"The thing is," Cody continued, "you're the most steadfast guy I know. If anyone can show her what real commitment looks like, it's you. But she's gotta be willing to see it."

Mitch sank into a chair opposite his brother. "She said I should seriously consider the offer, without any pressure from her."

"And will you? Consider it, I mean."

Would he? The offer represented professional recognition he'd never sought but couldn't help but appreciate. Yet, the mere thought of leaving Laurel Ridge—leaving Beth—created a physical ache in his chest.

"No." Mitch admitted finally. "I should consider it, though, shouldn't I?"

Cody shrugged. "Only you can answer that. But for what it's worth, I don't think you'd be happy in Charleston. You're not built for city life or bureaucracy. You're Laurel Ridge, through and through."

The simple observation resonated. Mitch was Laurel Ridge—its protector, its constant, its steady foundation. His entire identity was interwoven with this community, these mountains, these people.

Cody stood, gathering his papers. "Give her a little time to think through her reaction."

As his brother headed upstairs, Mitch remained at the kitchen table, his thoughts churning. The hurt of Beth's reaction hadn't diminished, but it was now tempered with understanding. He couldn't fault her for protecting herself from the pain she'd experienced before, even if it wounded him in the process.

***

Evening settled over the mountains, painting the western sky in deepening shades of orange and purple. Mitch sat on his front porch swing, the familiar creak a soothing rhythm beneath him. Duke lay at his feet, occasionally sighing contentedly.

Mitch's gaze swept across his property, taking in the fields that stretched toward the tree line, the barn his grandfather had built, the mountains that had witnessed generations of Bakers living and loving on this land. What would it mean to leave all this behind? To surrender his daily interactions with people he'd known his entire life? To abandon the community that had supported him through the darkest periods of his life?

And Beth. His heart constricted at the thought. What would it mean to walk away from the possibility of a future with her? From the chance to build a life with a woman who made him feel truly seen and wanted for the first time?

The equation was starkly clear: no professional achievement, no matter how prestigious, could compensate for losing Beth.

His feelings for her weren't fleeting or conditional—they had taken root in the deepest part of him. Her fear, while painful to witness, didn't diminish his love for her. If anything, it awakened a protective instinct that had always been central to his nature.

She was afraid of being abandoned again. Of being deemed insufficient, secondary to ambition. He needed to show her—not just tell her, but demonstrate through an unwavering presence—that she was enough. More than enough. She was everything.

The evening air cooled around him as stars began to appear overhead. Mitch closed his eyes, a prayer forming naturally in his mind.

Lord, give me wisdom. Show me how to reach Beth through her fear. Help her heart find peace, and guide me in bridging this distance between us. Let her see that my love isn't conditional or temporary. Give me patience and give her courage.

The prayer brought a measure of calm. His hurt hadn't disappeared, but it was now overlaid by a quiet, steadfast determination. He wouldn't let Beth's fear dictate their future. He'd give her space, but he wouldn't give up on them.

His decision about the FBI offer crystallized with perfect clarity. Charleston might offer professional advancement, but everything that truly mattered to him—everything that made his life worth living—was right here in Laurel Ridge. Most especially, Beth.

Mitch pulled out his phone, considering his approach carefully. He wouldn't push or demand. Beth needed reassurance, not pressure.

He typed a simple message: Beth I meant every word I said. I'm not going anywhere. This job offer changes nothing about how I feel or what I want. When you're ready to talk, I'll be here. Always.

He hit send, then pocketed his phone, letting out a long breath.

Whatever fears Beth was battling, whatever ghosts from her past were haunting her present, Mitch would be here. Steady. Patient. Unwavering. Just as he had been for his siblings, for his community, for everyone who had ever needed him.

The night deepened around the farmhouse, crickets joining in their nightly chorus. Mitch remained on the porch, the gentle motion of the swing matching the rhythm of his resolve. Some things were worth waiting for. Some people were worth fighting for.

Beth was both.

Chapter 23

Beth jerked awake in the pre-dawn stillness, her heart hammering against her ribs. No specific nightmare had startled her from sleep—just the persistent, looming dread that had settled over her since yesterday afternoon in Mitch's office. She lay still, staring at the ceiling where shadows played in the dim grayness filtering through her curtains.

Charleston. The word echoed in her mind, cold and accusatory.

The FBI wanted Mitch. She should feel proud of him, shouldn't she? Instead, all she felt was the icy grip of fear around her heart.

The light blanket, usually a comfort, felt heavy and constraining. Beth kicked it off and swung her legs over the side of the bed. The floorboards were cool beneath her bare feet as she padded to the window and drew back the curtains.

Outside, Laurel Ridge slumbered in the half-light of approaching dawn. The sky was painted in shades of indigo and charcoal, with just a hint of silver on the horizon. Her garden, usually a source of peaceful contemplation, looked ghostly and unfamiliar in the strange light.

Like everything else in her life right now.

Beth's phone lay face-down on her nightstand. She had left it set to silent all night. Now, with trembling fingers, she reached for it.

Beth, please call me. I don't understand what just happened. We need to talk about this.

Beth, I don't know what happened, but please don't shut me out. Whatever you're thinking, whatever you're afraid of, we can talk about it. I'm not going anywhere.

Beth, I meant every word I said. I'm not going anywhere. This job offer changes nothing about how I feel or what I want. When you're ready to talk, I'll be here. Always.

I'm not going anywhere. The phrase repeated in her mind, tangling with another memory—Matt, sitting across their kitchen table last summer, saying, "You know I'll always be here for you, babe," while his phone buzzed with messages, probably from the woman who would replace her.

Words were easy. Actions were what mattered. And the action she'd witnessed was Mitch considering an offer in Charleston—the very city that had lured Matt away.

But... had she really witnessed that? Or had she simply heard what she feared?

Beth set the phone down and pressed her palms against her eyes, which felt raw and gritty from a restless sleep.

"Did I even give him a chance to explain?" she whispered into the empty room.

The house answered with oppressive silence.

In the kitchen, Beth went through the motions of her morning routine. She measured the coffee grounds into the filter, filled the reservoir with water, and pressed the button to brew. The familiar gurgle of the coffee maker provided a small comfort in the growing light of dawn.

She leaned against the counter, arms wrapped around herself, replaying yesterday's scene for the hundredth time.

They want me to head it up. Based in Charleston.

The logical part of her brain knew Mitch wasn't Matt. Mitch had been nothing but honest, consistent, and trustworthy since she'd known him.

But logic had little power against the visceral memory of betrayal.

The coffee maker beeped, signaling completion, but Beth made no move to pour herself a cup. The rich aroma that usually energized her now made her stomach clench.

I've never imagined working anywhere but here. My life is here.

The coffee grew cold as Beth stood motionless, caught in the riptide of her thoughts.

"Mitch isn't Matt," she said aloud, her voice sounding strange in the quiet kitchen.

Her eyes fell on the calendar hanging beside the refrigerator. Bible study had been last night—the one she'd skipped, too overwhelmed by her emotions to face a room full of people who might notice her distress. Had Mitch gone? Had he looked for her? The thought sent a pang of guilt through her chest.

Beth poured herself a cup of coffee, more out of habit than desire. She took a sip and grimaced. It tasted flat and bitter, nothing like the comforting warmth it usually provided.

She carried the mug to her bedroom to get dressed for work. As she opened her closet, a flash of burgundy caught her eye—the dress she'd worn to River Bend Vineyard, hanging at the end of the rack where she'd placed it to be dry-cleaned.

Beth reached out, her fingers brushing the soft fabric. The memory of that evening rushed back with startling clarity—the music flowing around them, the lights reflecting in Mitch's eyes as he told her he was falling in love with her, the certainty she'd felt when returning those words.

Had that been real?

She yanked her hand back as if the dress had burned her, then grabbed the first items she found—a navy blouse and tan slacks that would require minimal thought.

In the bathroom, Beth caught sight of her reflection and barely recognized herself. Her eyes were shadowed by dark circles, her complexion pale, her expression haunted.

"I look like I've been dragged through a hedge backward," she murmured, splashing cold water on her face in a futile attempt to restore some vitality.

The enormity of what had happened—what might be happening—settled heavily on her shoulders. She wasn't just losing a potential relationship; she was losing the renewed sense of possibility that had been blooming within her since Mitch entered her life.

Beth closed her eyes.

"God, I don't understand. Why is this happening? Am I supposed to trust him? How can I risk this again?" Her prayer felt fractured, desperate. "Show me a sign, anything. Did I jump to conclusions too quickly? I believe I did, but I need help to fix what I've done and figure out how to move forward and trust."

The prayer brought no immediate peace, no sudden clarity. Just the hollow echo of her fears.

She finished getting ready mechanically, brushing her teeth, applying minimal makeup to conceal the evidence of her sleepless night, pulling her hair into a simple ponytail.

As she gathered her purse and keys, Beth paused by the kitchen table where her Bible lay. She'd missed last night's study, but perhaps Scripture could offer what her own anxious thoughts could not.

She flipped it open to where her bookmark was, her eyes falling on a passage from Proverbs: "Trust in the Lord with all your heart and lean not on your own understanding; in all your ways submit to him, and he will make your paths straight."

Trust.

The word both comforted and challenged her. Trust in God, yes—but what about trust in Mitch? In her own judgment? The lines had blurred dangerously.

Her phone buzzed with a morning alarm reminder. Mountain Chic opened in an hour, and despite her emotional turmoil, she had responsibilities.

With a deep breath, she straightened her shoulders and headed for the door. Work would provide structure, normalcy, and a temporary refuge from the storm of her thoughts.

Chapter 24

Mitch stared into his coffee cup, the once-steaming liquid now cold and forgotten. Martha's Saturday morning special—two eggs over easy, bacon, hash browns, and a biscuit—sat barely touched on the plate before him. The usual weekend chatter of Martha's Diner faded to a distant hum, overwhelmed by the endless loop of yesterday's scene playing in his mind.

The look in Beth's eyes. That was what haunted him the most. Not anger or disappointment, but raw, undiluted fear.

"Charleston." Her voice had trembled on the word, and in that moment, he'd watched her retreat behind invisible walls, her trust in him crumbling before his eyes.

Mitch pushed the plate away and ran a hand over his face. The bell above the diner door jangled and Mitch turned to see who had entered... just a family of six.

"Excuse me, Sheriff?" The father approached, map in hand. "Could you point us toward the trailhead for Eagle Rock? We've been driving in circles."

Mitch straightened, years of public service overriding his personal turmoil. "Sure thing." He pointed to a spot on their map. "You're actually not far. Take River Road north about three miles, then watch for the brown park sign on your right. Can't miss it."

"Thanks so much," the man replied, returning to his family.

Mitch's shoulders slumped as the automatic smile faded from his face. He returned to staring at his coffee, his thumb absently tracing the rim of the mug.

The FBI job offer itself didn't tempt him. His life was in Laurel Ridge; his heart was with Beth. But that didn't matter if she couldn't believe it.

"You planning on drinking that coffee?" Martha asked, her tone gentle despite the teasing words.

Mitch glanced up, offering a weak smile that didn't reach his eyes. "Sorry, Martha. Mind's elsewhere this morning."

Martha studied him, her gaze sharp and knowing. Without a word, she poured herself a cup of coffee, wiped her hands on her blue-checkered apron, and came around the counter. She settled onto the stool beside him with a quiet sigh, her knees cracking slightly as she sat.

"You know," she said conversationally, "I've been serving you breakfast since you were a gangly deputy with a bad haircut. And in all those years, I've never seen you leave food on your plate like this." She patted his arm, her touch warm and motherly. "You're a thousand miles away this morning, Mitch. And that plate of food isn't that bad, is it? Want to tell an old woman what's weighing so heavy on those shoulders of yours?"

The genuine concern in her voice cracked something in Mitch's carefully maintained composure. He glanced around the diner—the tourist family was occupied with looking at menus. The only other customers were an elderly couple in the far corner, and the other waitress was busy in the kitchen. It was as private as the diner would get.

He exhaled heavily, his shoulders dropping. "I'm not sure where to even start, Martha."

"The beginning usually works," she suggested as she took a sip of her coffee. "Or just the part that's sitting like a stone in your gut. Talking helps clear the fog sometimes, son."

Mitch trusted Martha implicitly. She'd been a constant in his life since childhood, had helped him through the darkest days after his mother left. If anyone could offer perspective, it was her.

"I got a job offer yesterday," he began, his voice low. "The FBI wants me to head up a new rural crimes task force. Based in Charleston."

Martha's eyebrows rose slightly, but she remained silent, letting him continue.

"Beth came by the office just as I was finishing the call. She... I told her about the job offer." Mitch's fingers tightened around his mug. "And Martha, it was like watching a light go out. She heard 'Charleston' and it was like... like a lightning bolt had struck her. I saw it in her eyes. She wasn't seeing me anymore. She was seeing him."

"Matt," Martha supplied quietly.

"Yeah. At least that's what I've figured out so far," Mitch nodded. "I told her I couldn't see myself leaving Laurel Ridge, especially not now. But she wouldn't hear it. Said I needed space to consider the offer without her 'clouding my judgment.' Then she just... left."

The memory of Beth's retreating sent a fresh wave of pain through him. "I've texted her, tried to explain, but she's not responding. I told her I wasn't going anywhere."

Martha listened intently, her weathered face softening with understanding. She reached over and covered his hand with her own.

"Oh, Mitch." She shook her head slowly. "Charleston for that dear girl... that city isn't just a place; it's a wound that's been ripped open fresh again. Matt Rutledge didn't just break her heart; he shattered her. It's a terrible thing when you can't trust yourself to see the truth."

Mitch shifted on his stool as raw emotion coursed through him.

"I just don't understand how she could think I'd do the same thing," he admitted, the hurt evident in his voice. "After everything we've shared, after telling each other how we feel... how could she not know me better than that?"

Martha sighed, her expression tender but firm. "It's not about knowing you, Mitch. It's about believing she can trust what she thinks she knows. Matt always gave her pretty words and, in the end, left her feeling insecure and unworthy. For her, this isn't about logic—it's about survival."

She took a sip of her coffee before continuing. "She's heard promises before, son. Words can be cheap, especially when fear is shouting louder. Right now, your words, no matter how true, might sound like echoes of his lies to her. She needs to see your truth, and feel it, unwavering and steady."

"So what do you suggest, oh wise one?" he asked, his voice rougher than intended. "Just... wait? Hope she comes around?"

Martha's eyes crinkled at the corners, her expression thoughtful. "Mitch, this is gonna be like trying to coax a deer that's been hunted. You can't rush this. You can't chase after her, demanding she trust you. You just have to be still and patient. Let her realize there's no threat in you, only gentleness."

She stirred her coffee slowly; the spoon clinking against the ceramic. "You pray on this, Mitch. Pray for her heart to find peace, and for God to give you the patience of Job. Remember what the Good Book says about love? 'It bears all things, believes all things, hopes all things, endures all things.' That 'endures' part... that's where the real work of love lies, especially when fear builds walls around someone."

The Scripture resonated in Mitch's heart. Love endures. Not just the easy moments of connection and joy, but the painful misunderstandings, the fear, the doubt.

"I don't intend to push her," he said quietly. "But I don't want her thinking I've given up, either."

"Then find the middle ground," Martha advised. "Give her space, but make sure she knows you're still there. Not with grand gestures or desperate pleas—those might just scare her more. But with small, consistent reminders that you're not going anywhere. That, unlike Matt, you're a man of your word. And for heaven's sakes... approach this with good ole conversation and presence."

Mitch nodded slowly, considering. "You really think she'll come around?"

Martha's gaze turned fierce, surprising him with its intensity. "Beth Rutledge is a strong woman. That girl rebuilt her entire life after that worthless man left her. She didn't just survive; she thrived. She's got courage in spades, Mitch. She's just forgotten it for a moment."

She squeezed his hand. "She'll see it, Mitch. She'll see you're not him. But you can't force her eyes open. You just have to be the light that's there when she's ready to look."

Something loosened in Mitch's chest at Martha's words—not the ache itself, but the constriction of helplessness that had accompanied it. This wasn't about convincing Beth with clever arguments or impassioned pleas. It was about being steady, being himself, and giving her time to trust herself again.

He took a sip of coffee, its warmth spreading through him. "The job in Charleston..." He shook his head decisively. "Martha, there's no decision to make. It was never a choice. I'd walk away from a thousand promotions before I'd walk away from the chance of a life with her. The problem is making her believe that when she's so convinced history is repeating itself."

Martha's face broke into a gentle smile. "You show her, dear. Every day, in every small way, you show her. Steadfastness speaks louder than any grand declaration when a heart is frightened."

Mitch picked up his fork and took a bite of his now-cold eggs, his appetite returning slightly with the clarity Martha had provided.

"I'm going to formally turn down the FBI offer on Monday," he said between bites. "No need to drag that out."

Martha tilted her head. "You're sure that's what you want? It's quite an honor, Mitch."

"I'm sure." His voice held absolute conviction. "My life is here. Everything that matters to me is in Laurel Ridge." He set his fork down, meeting Martha's gaze directly. "I love her, Martha. More than I thought possible. These past few weeks with Beth have shown me what I've been missing—not just romantically, but in really living, in sharing myself with someone. I'm not about to throw that away for a title and an office in Charleston."

Martha's eyes glistened. "Well then. Seems to me Beth Rutledge is a very lucky woman, whether she realizes it yet or not."

Mitch gave a half-smile, tinged with sadness. "I just hope she gives me the chance to prove it."

"Have faith, Mitch," Martha replied, her voice softening. "In God's timing and in Beth's heart. Sometimes the detours in love's journey are what make the destination all the sweeter when you finally arrive."

She glanced at the customers by the register. "Now, I'd better get back to work before those customers start giving me the stink eye." She stood, patting his shoulder affectionately. "You finish that breakfast.

Sheriff or not, I won't have you passing out from hunger on my watch."

Mitch caught her hand before she could walk away. "Thanks, Martha. I love you, you know that, right?"

Her face softened with genuine affection. "And I love you. You've got a good heart, Mitchell Baker. And a strong back. You'll weather this. Just keep praying and keep loving."

As Martha returned to her duties, Mitch found himself able to finish most of his breakfast. The pain hadn't disappeared—the ache of Beth's absence still throbbed steadily—but Martha's wisdom had given him a path forward. Not a quick solution, but a sustainable approach rooted in patience and unwavering commitment.

He paid his bill, leaving Martha a generous tip, and stepped out into the bright Saturday morning.

Mitch's gaze traveled automatically to Mountain Chic, two doors down. The boutique's windows gleamed in the morning sun, mannequins showcasing Beth's keen eye for style. Was she in there now? His instinct was to walk straight to her, to try again to make her understand. But Martha's words echoed in his mind: *You can't rush it. You can't chase after it, demanding it trust you.*

Instead, Mitch turned toward his truck.

She was worth waiting for. Worth fighting for. Worth enduring for.

Chapter 25

Beth emerged from her office wearing the hiking clothes she kept in her office—moisture-wicking leggings and a lightweight blue tank top.

"I need to clear my head," she announced to Pearl and Alisha as she walked to the front door of the store, slinging a small backpack over her shoulder. "I'm leaving early. Close up the shop without me."

Pearl's forehead creased with concern. "Honey, are you all right?"

"I'm fine," Beth insisted, the words automatic. "I just need some fresh air and exercise. I'll see you both on Monday."

She strode out, water bottle clutched in her hand, before either woman could question her further. The late afternoon sun beat down on Main Street, the July heat wrapping around her like a heavy blanket. She crossed the street quickly, barely registering the familiar storefronts and passing faces that usually brought her joy.

Her pace was brisk, almost frantic, as she headed toward the swinging bridge that connected the town to the wilderness trails beyond.

The wooden planks creaked beneath her feet as she crossed, the gentle sway of the bridge over the New River providing no comfort today.

As she reached the end of the bridge, Beth paused only long enough to consider which trail to take. The Endurance Trail. Four miles. Moderate to difficult. Perfect.

The trail began immediately with an upward slope, the dirt path winding its way between towering oaks and pines. Beth attacked it with single-minded determination, pushing her legs to climb faster than prudence would dictate. The physical exertion was a relief—something tangible to focus on instead of the emotional storm within.

Twenty minutes in, sweat dampened her tank top and her breath came in sharp pulls. The trail had become steeper, with occasional rough stone steps embedded in the dirt. Beth welcomed the challenge, the burn in her thighs and calves a distraction from the constant replay of yesterday's scene in Mitch's office.

That was William Davis, Assistant Director of the FBI's Criminal Division...

Beth pushed harder up a particularly steep section, her boots digging into the soft earth for traction.

They want me to head it up. Based in Charleston.

Her lungs protested the pace, but she ignored the discomfort, focusing instead on the rhythm of her feet against the trail.

Charleston.

"Stop it," Beth muttered aloud, startling a nearby chickadee into flight. She paused, hands on knees, drawing deep breaths as sweat trickled down her temples.

A hiker descending the trail nodded in greeting as he passed. "Careful up ahead," he cautioned. "Trail gets pretty steep before the waterfall."

Beth thanked him automatically, then straightened.

As she continued climbing, the forest grew denser, the canopy overhead filtering the sunlight into dappled patterns on the forest floor. The distant sound of rushing water gradually became audible, growing louder with each step forward.

Mitch isn't Matt. I didn't even give him a chance. I heard Charleston, and I bolted.

Her pace slowed as the trail narrowed, winding along the edge of a steep incline. The roar of the waterfall grew louder, drawing her forward. When the trail curved sharply to the right, the trees parted to reveal a clearing, and Beth stopped short, momentarily awed by the sight before her.

The powerful waterfall cascaded down a rock face about thirty feet high, the white water crashing into a clear pool below before continuing as a stream that disappeared into the forest. Sunlight caught the spray, creating tiny rainbows that danced in the mist.

Beth approached the pool, her hiking boots crunching on the mix of stones and sand that ringed the water. The cool spray from the waterfall touched her overheated skin, a welcome relief after the strenuous climb. On impulse, she set down her backpack and water bottle, and removed her boots and socks.

She waded into the shallow pool at the base of the fall, the cold water immediately cooling her ankles. The sensation was bracing, and real, pulling her firmly into the present moment instead of the loop of regret that had consumed her since yesterday.

A large, flat rock jutted out into the pool, warmed by the filtered sunlight. Beth carefully made her way to it, stepping carefully on the slippery stones beneath the water's surface. When she reached the rock, she hoisted herself up and lay back, the sun-warmed stone seeping heat into her tired muscles while the cool mist from the waterfall kissed her face.

The sensory contrast grounded her, creating a momentary stillness in her mind.

"I panicked," she admitted to herself out loud, staring up at the blue sky overhead. "I heard Charleston, and I panicked."

She hadn't reacted to Mitch at all—she'd reacted to the ghost of Matt, to the memory of betrayal that still haunted her.

"It was Matt I was seeing," she whispered aloud, her voice lost in the roar of the waterfall. "Matt, I was reacting to. Not Mitch."

A wave of anger surged through her—not at Mitch, but at Matt for the long shadow his betrayal had cast, and at herself for letting it continue to dictate her.

"I'm so tired of him having this power over me," she said, the words coming out harsh and clear.

She forced herself to recall Mitch's actions over the weeks they'd known gotten closer: his steady presence during the boutique theft; his gentle patience during Bible study; his genuine delight in her success with the children's store lease; the way he'd looked at her as they danced at River Bend Vineyard, his eyes full of love.

Then she remembered the hurt and confusion on his face when she'd pulled back in his office, the way his texts had grown increasingly concerned, then gentle, and then accepting of her silence.

He's shown me who he is, over and over. And I threw it back in his face because I was scared.

A deep ache of regret settled in her chest. "I have to fix this," she whispered. "I owe him an apology."

The admission opened something in her, a dam breaking after months—years—of careful control. She began to speak aloud, her voice a raw whisper against the backdrop of the waterfall.

"God, I messed up. I really messed up."

The words tumbled out, gathering momentum like the water cascading down the surrounding rocks.

"I was so scared. I just reacted. I let Matt's shadow dictate everything. I didn't trust You, and I didn't trust Mitch, and I didn't even trust myself to see clearly."

Her eyes stung with unshed tears as she stared up at the sky through the veil of mist.

"I want what I've witnessed with Mitch—that partnership, that understanding, that safety. Is it too late? Did I push him away for good?"

The question hung in the air, unanswered. The waterfall continued its steady roar, indifferent to her pain.

"Please, Lord, show me what to do. Help me to let go of this fear. Help me to trust again—to trust Your leading, and to trust the good man You've put in my path."

Her voice broke on the last words, tears finally spilling over to trace warm paths down her temples and into her hair.

"Help me to be brave enough to make this right."

For several minutes, Beth lay still, spent from her emotional outpouring, her eyes gazing upward. The tension gradually eased from her body, replaced by a hollow emptiness that wasn't quite peace but no longer held the sharp edges of her earlier distress.

A flicker of movement caught her attention. Something vibrant darted through the air above her—a butterfly, its wings a brilliant orange and black pattern that identified it as a monarch. It flitted and danced in the space above her, its delicate form catching the sunlight as it wove an intricate pattern through the mist.

Beth watched its progress, momentarily mesmerized by the creature's graceful movements. Then, gently, impossibly, it landed right on her chest, just above her heart. Its delicate wings fanned slowly open and closed, the vibrant orange seeming to glow against the blue of her tank top.

She held perfectly still, afraid to breathe too deeply, lest she disturb the fragile visitor. The world around her seemed to pause, the constant roar of the waterfall receding in her awareness until all that existed was this moment—this tiny creature resting trustingly against her.

A verse floated into her mind, clear and insistent: "Therefore, if anyone is in Christ, the new creation has come: The old has gone, the new is here."

The butterfly was a living embodiment of transformation—once bound by limitations, now free to soar. Just as she had been praying to let go of the old—her fear, Matt's influence—and embrace the new—a future with Mitch, trust, and healing.

The butterfly's appearance felt like a touch from God, an answer to her plea, a moment of profound peace amidst her storm. It was a sign that He was with her, that He heard her.

As the butterfly rested there, Beth felt a tiny seed of hope unfurl within her. When it finally took to the air again, wings carrying it effortlessly upward, she felt a sense of release, as if it were carrying some of her burden with it.

Beth watched until the butterfly disappeared. The tears on her face had dried, and though a faint ache of regret still lingered, the despair that had driven her up the mountain was gone, replaced by a quiet, burgeoning resolve.

She sat up slowly on the rock, trailing her fingers through the cold water surrounding it. It felt cleansing and cool. The warmth of the rock beneath her felt like a steady foundation.

She knew what she needed to do. The fear hadn't vanished entirely, but her courage now felt stronger, and more substantial. She had allowed Matt's betrayal to become a lens through which she viewed all relationships. It was time to set that lens aside and see clearly.

As she waded through the water and began putting her socks and boots back on, a plan began to form. Not just an apology, but a genuine opening of herself—fears, hopes, and all—to the man who had consistently shown himself worthy of her trust.

The trek back down the mountain would be easier physically, but the journey she was preparing to undertake—the one back to Mitch, back to vulnerability, back to hope—would require a different kind of courage entirely.

Beth shouldered her backpack, took one last look at the waterfall that had witnessed her breakdown and her breakthrough, and turned toward the trail. A smile curved her lips as she began the descent, each step feeling lighter than the last.

Chapter 26

Beth's fingers trembled as she gripped the heavy brass handle of the church door. Inside, the opening strains of "Amazing Grace" swelled—each familiar note both welcoming and terrifying. She stood frozen, her Sunday dress sticking to her skin despite the early morning coolness.

I can do this. I have to do this.

The monarch butterfly from yesterday flashed in her mind—its delicate orange wings against her heart. That tiny moment of grace at the waterfall had propelled her here.

She pulled the door open and slipped inside, letting the door close softly behind her. The vestibule provided momentary shelter, a liminal space between retreat and commitment. She could see the backs of heads—familiar hairstyles and Sunday hats, parents with arms around children's shoulders, elderly couples leaning together.

The aisle between the pews stretched before her like an impossible journey, longer than she remembered, every step requiring conscious effort. She walked forward, her heels clicking softly against the wooden floor, the sound swallowed by the congregation's singing.

Her focus narrowed as she scanned the pews. There—three rows from the front on the right side—sat Mitch, flanked by Tessa and Cody. His broad shoulders were set in a straight line, his attention fixed forward. Even from behind, she could read the tension in his posture, the careful rigidity that hadn't been there before.

I put that there. I did that to him.

Beth walked down the aisle, her pace measured. Not rushing, not hesitating. Her heartbeat thundered in her ears, nearly drowning out the final strains of the hymn. As the congregation settled back into their seats, she reached his pew.

"Excuse me," she whispered to the elderly man at the end.

He shifted, allowing her to pass. Three more people moved their knees. Four spaces to navigate. Tessa looked up, her eyes widening. She touched Cody's arm, and he too glanced up, surprise evident on his face as he scooted over to make room for her.

Beth sat down beside Mitch, the wood of the pew hard beneath her. He stiffened as her presence registered. Beth didn't look at his face—couldn't bear to yet. Instead, she placed her hand over his where it rested on his leg.

For three terrible heartbeats, his hand remained still. Then, slowly, he turned his hand and his fingers curled around hers.

Pastor Andrew's voice filled the sanctuary, welcoming the congregation and announcing the morning scripture. Beth couldn't process the words. The entire world had narrowed to the point of contact between her hand and Mitch's.

"Our text today comes from Hebrews, chapter 11," Pastor Andrew's voice floated above her internal chaos. "'Now faith is confidence in what we hope for and assurance about what we do not see.'"

Faith. Of course, it would be about faith today.

The sermon unfolded around them, words about stepping into the unknown, about trusting when every logical impulse screamed caution. Beth tried to focus, to find meaning in the pastor's message, but her awareness kept snapping back to Mitch's hand beneath hers.

Had his fingers tightened slightly? Was that tension or reassurance? She couldn't look at him, couldn't bear to see rejection or worse—pity—in those brown eyes that had looked at her with such tenderness just days ago.

So she kept her gaze forward, on the cross hanging above the altar, on the stained-glass depicting a shepherd with a lamb across his shoulders. She sat straight-backed, her breathing deliberately steady, her exterior calm betraying none of the earthquake happening within.

The service progressed through its familiar rhythm—prayers, scripture, hymns, responsive readings. Each element passed in a blur, the congregation's voices rising and falling like distant waves. Beth participated automatically, her lips forming responses by rote while her mind screamed questions she couldn't voice.

What will he say when we can finally speak? Have I destroyed everything? Is there anything left to save?

As the final hymn concluded and Pastor Andrew offered the benediction, movement rippled through the sanctuary. People stood, gathering purses and Bibles, children squirming free from parental hands, conversations beginning in hushed tones.

Mitch began to rise. Beth tightened her grip on his hand, the gentle pressure a silent plea: Wait. Please.

Their eyes met for the first time—a fleeting connection, electric and uncertain. She couldn't read his expression, couldn't tell if the carefully neutral mask he wore concealed anger or hope.

She held his gaze, letting her desperation show.

Please stay.

Around them, the congregation filed out row by row. Beth was acutely aware of curious glances, of Tessa's questioning look at their joined hands, of Cody's slight nod to his brother before following his sister down the aisle.

Martha passed by, her face softening as she caught Beth's eye. She offered a small, encouraging smile before continuing toward the exit.

The sanctuary emptied steadily—footsteps on hardwood, murmured greetings, the occasional laugh from the gathering space beyond. The heavy doors at the back of the sanctuary opened and closed in a steady rhythm until, finally, they thudded shut behind the last departing family.

Silence descended, vast and profound, broken only by the gentle hum of the building's air conditioning and Beth's own unsteady breathing.

They sat side by side in the empty sanctuary, sun streaming through the stained-glass, casting jeweled patterns across the worn wood of the pews. The colored light fell across their joined hands—ruby red, sapphire blue, emerald green—transforming something ordinary into something sacred.

Beth turned to face him fully, not letting go of his hand. She had rehearsed words on her solitary hike back from the waterfall, composed speeches during her sleepless night, and practiced apologies in her bathroom mirror that morning. None of those careful phrases came to her now.

"Mitch..." Her voice came out stronger than she expected, steadier than she felt. "I... I am so profoundly sorry. For how I acted. For what I assumed. For the pain I know I caused you. I messed up. I made a mistake."

His face remained carefully neutral, but his eyes—those warm brown eyes—watched her with an intensity that made her skin prickle.

"I heard you on the phone before I even stepped in your office," she continued, the words coming faster now. "When you said 'Charleston'... it was like a switch flipped inside me." Beth swallowed hard. "Then after I was in your office, and you explained about the call... suddenly, I wasn't in your office anymore. I was back with Matt, hearing his lies. And I reacted out of fear."

Tears burned behind her eyes. She blinked them back, determined to get through this without breaking down completely.

"I went hiking yesterday, trying to make sense of how I reacted and what I did. And I just... I broke. I told God I was so tired of Matt having this power over me, of letting his betrayal poison everything good in my life."

Her free hand moved to her heart, pressing against the spot where the butterfly had rested.

"And then... there was this butterfly, Mitch. It just landed right here." Her fingers splayed across her chest. "It felt... like God was telling me the old had to go, that there was a chance for something new. For us."

Mitch's hand shifted beneath hers, his thumb brushing against her wrist in the slightest caress. The small movement sent hope spiraling through her.

"Your texts..." Beth's voice caught. "You said you weren't going anywhere. That you wanted to talk. And all I did was shut you out." A tear escaped despite her efforts, tracking down her cheek. "I am so sorry for not trusting you, for not believing in the good, honest man you are."

She drew a shaky breath, reaching for the words that mattered most.

"What we have... what I feel for you... it's real, Mitch. It's more real and precious than anything I've ever known. And I almost threw it all away because I was terrified." Her voice broke, vulnerability raw in every syllable. "I love you. I love your kindness, your strength, the way you make me feel safe, even when I'm falling apart inside."

She didn't wipe away the tears that trailed down her face.

"I don't know if you can forgive me for my blindness, for my fear. But I had to come. I had to tell you." Her fingers tightened around his. "I want to try, Mitch. If you'll let me. I want to trust us. One day at a time. Or even one breath at a time, if that's what it takes."

Her voice dropped to a whisper, raw and pleading. "I just... I don't want to lose you."

The words hung in the air between them. Her soul laid bare in the silent sanctuary. Beth watched his face, searching for any sign—forgiveness, rejection, hesitation—anything that would tell her if she'd destroyed everything they'd begun to build.

Silence stretched between them, filled with the weight of all she'd confessed. Each second felt like an eternity, each breath a lifetime. Her hand in his was her only anchor in the storm of uncertainty.

Please, God, please. Let it not be too late.

Mitch hadn't pulled away, hadn't left. That had to mean something, didn't it? Or was he simply being kind, preparing to let her down gently?

Beth waited, suspended between hope and fear, for his response.

Chapter 27

Mitch felt the tremor in Beth's hand where it gripped his and saw the tears making glittery tracks down her cheeks.

I don't want to lose you.

Her last plea echoed against the empty pews, resonating through the quiet church like the fading note of a bell. Mitch sat perfectly still, his chest tight with a storm of emotions too powerful and too complex to immediately voice.

Her hand in his felt small, fragile, yet her grip was fierce, as if she were hanging on for dear life. Through their connected palms, he could feel her pulse racing.

Her eyes—those expressive hazel-green eyes that had captivated him from the beginning—searched his face with desperate hope warring against profound fear.

Martha's words from yesterday returned with crystalline clarity: *For that dear girl, Charleston isn't just a place; it's a wound that's been ripped open fresh again.*

Beth had come to him. Despite her fear, despite the voice of past betrayal whispering poisonous doubts, she had walked down that church aisle, sat beside him, had taken his hand, and never once let go. The courage that must have required humbled him beyond measure.

He'd prayed for a bridge across the chasm between them, and here she was, building it with her trembling hands and tear-soaked words. An answer to prayer, sitting beside him in a puddle of colored light through the windows.

Words felt impossibly inadequate. How could mere syllables possibly convey the depth of what he felt at this moment?

Slowly, with a reverence that made the gesture almost sacred, Mitch lifted his free hand to her face. His palm, rough from years of work, cradled her cheek with infinite gentleness. His thumb brushed away a fresh tear, the moisture cool against his skin.

Beth's eyes fluttered closed briefly at his touch, a shaky breath escaping her lips. When she opened them again, they shone with a fragile, newborn hope.

"Beth..." His voice emerged thick with emotion, slightly hoarse, as if the word had to force its way past the knot in his throat.

Her name contained multitudes: relief, tenderness, pain, and, above all, love.

"Oh, Beth." He squeezed her fingers gently. "Charleston... Matt... I understand. Or at least, I'm beginning to." He drew a steadying breath. "I realized it wasn't about you not trusting me. It was about him, and that deep wound he left in your heart."

"Friday..." Mitch paused, knowing he needed to acknowledge his hurt without making her bear the weight of it. "Yes, you're walking away hurt. More than I can say. Because for quite a few awful hours, I thought I'd lost the most precious, unexpected gift I'd ever been given."

A small, fresh tear escaped from the corner of her eye. Mitch caught it with his thumb, his touch feather-light against her skin.

"But that butterfly, Beth?" A wondering smile touched his lips. "The one that landed on your heart? I think God sent that for both of us. A reminder that new beginnings are real. That transformation is possible."

He shifted slightly on the hard wooden pew, turning more fully toward her, their knees nearly touching.

"The FBI job…" He shook his head, the gesture decisive, almost dismissive. "Sweetheart, there was never a choice to make." His gaze held hers steadily. "My 'serious consideration' was mostly figuring out how to tell an Assistant Director of the FBI 'no' without sounding like a completely ungrateful fool. My heart, my future, Beth… it's always been here. In Laurel Ridge." He met her eyes, his gaze unwavering. "With you."

Her lips parted in a silent gasp, the beginnings of relief starting to soften the tight lines of anxiety around her eyes.

"Those texts I sent? Every single word was the truest thing I knew. I am not going anywhere." His voice strengthened with absolute conviction. "You don't cloud my judgment, Beth. You are my judgment. You're my clarity, my best direction."

He squeezed her hand gently, the pressure an affirmation of his words. "You said you love my kindness, my strength… Beth, you make me want to be stronger, kinder. You make me a better man. Just by being you."

A sob caught in Beth's throat, not of pain but of overwhelming emotion. "Mitch, I—"

"Shh," he whispered, his expression tender. He brought their joined hands to his lips, pressing a lingering kiss against her knuckles. The church air felt cool against his heated skin, the distant hum of the building's air conditioning a gentle counterpoint to their ragged breathing.

"One day at a time?" he echoed her earlier words softly. "Or one breath at a time, like you said? Then that's what we'll do. We'll take each breath, and each day, together." His voice dropped lower, infused with solemn promise. "And I promise you, Beth, I'll do everything in my power to show you that my love is real, that I'm worthy of your trust, and that your heart is completely safe with me."

Mitch released her hand, only to frame her face between both of his palms. His touch was reverent, as if holding something infinitely precious. The tears on her cheeks dampened his fingers as he drew her closer, their foreheads coming to rest against each other.

"I love you, Beth Rutledge," he whispered, his voice raw with emotion, meant for her ears alone. "More than I ever imagined, it was possible to love someone. And the thought of losing you..." His voice broke slightly, the admission pulling from somewhere deep within. "That's just not a possibility I'm willing to accept."

He pulled back just enough to look deeply into her eyes, seeing her tears now mingling with dawning joy, with relief so profound it seemed to radiate from her like physical warmth.

"You asked if it's too late," he murmured, his thumbs stroking her cheeks. "It is never too late for what's true, Beth."

Mitch leaned forward, closing the last breath of space between them. His lips met hers with exquisite tenderness—not the passionate kiss from the vineyard, nor the playful one from their picnic. This was a different kind of communion altogether. A sealing of promises. A forgiveness of hurts. A welcome home.

He kissed her slowly, gently, putting every unspoken vow into the pressure of his mouth against hers. Her tears tasted salty on his lips, but the sweetness of reunion overwhelmed everything else. Her hands came up to rest against his chest, fingers curling slightly into the fabric of his shirt as if to anchor herself to him.

When they parted, Beth's eyes remained closed for a moment, her expression one of profound peace. When she opened them, Mitch saw what he'd been searching for—the fear was gone, replaced by quiet certainty.

He drew her against him. She nestled closer, her head finding the hollow of his shoulder as if the space had been crafted just for her. He rested his cheek against her hair, breathing in the faint floral scent of her shampoo, letting the reality of their reconciliation settle around them like a blessing.

Colored light bathed them from the windows, the empty sanctuary a cathedral to their private redemption. Mitch's gaze lifted to the cross hanging above the altar, gratitude welling within him.

"Pastor Andrew was right this morning," he said, his voice rumbling in his chest beneath her ear. "Faith is confidence in what we hope for and assurance about what we do not see. And all I've hoped for, all I've prayed for since I truly saw you..." He gestured gently between them. "Is this. Us. Together."

Beth lifted her head to look at him, her smile watery but radiant. "I almost let fear rob me of this."

"But you didn't," Mitch reminded her, tucking a strand of hair behind her ear. "You came back. You fought through it. That's courage, Beth. That's faith."

"How did you know?" she asked, searching his face. "How did you know not to give up on me?"

Mitch's expression softened. "Because I know you. The real you—not the scared you, not the wounded you, but the core of who you are. And that woman? She's worth waiting for. Worth fighting for."

He shifted slightly, reaching into his pocket and withdrawing a small, folded paper. "I was going to give this to Leslie to give to you if you didn't come today. I wasn't sure if you would."

"What is it?" Beth asked, eyeing the paper curiously.

"A copy of my letter to the FBI." He unfolded it carefully, revealing the formal letterhead and his signature at the bottom. "I wrote it yesterday. I plan to mail it Monday morning."

Beth's eyes widened. "But... you hadn't even talked to me yet. You didn't know if..."

"Hush... the job was never meant for me. But more importantly—" he refolded the letter, tapping it against his palm, "I choose Laurel Ridge. I choose this community, and this life. And I choose you, Beth."

The sanctuary air seemed to wrap around them, warm and still, holding this moment with all its fragile perfection. They could hear the distant sounds of the congregation outside—laughter, the clink of coffee cups, children's voices raised in play. Life continuing its steady rhythm.

"I should probably tell Tessa and Cody they can stop hovering in the vestibule," Mitch said with a small smile. "I saw them peeking in a few minutes ago."

Beth laughed, the sound like water over stones, washing away the last of the tension. "Let them hover. I don't mind."

"They're just worried about me," Mitch admitted. "They saw what Friday did to me."

"I'm so sorry," Beth whispered, her hand finding his cheek.

"No more apologies," Mitch said firmly. "From either of us. We're learning, Beth. Learning how to love each other. Learning how to trust. There will be missteps. What matters is that we find our way back... always."

She nodded, her expression solemn. "I'm learning how to untangle Matt's voice from my own fears. It's hard sometimes."

"I know," Mitch acknowledged. "And I'll be patient when those fears surface because they will. But I'll also be here to remind you of what's real." He took her hand, placing it over his heart. "This is real. My love for you isn't conditional on perfect understanding or never making mistakes."

Beth's eyes filled with fresh tears, but these were different—healing, cleansing. "No one has ever loved me like this."

"Get used to it," Mitch said, his voice light but his eyes serious. "Because I plan to love you like this for a very long time."

A peaceful silence settled between them, comfortable and profound.

"We should probably join the others," Beth said eventually, though she made no move to stand.

"Probably," Mitch agreed, equally reluctant to break their sanctuary. "Martha will have questions. And knowing this town..."

Beth winced slightly. "Gossip?"

"Care," Mitch corrected gently. "This community loves you, Beth, and they love me. They've been worried. Martha especially."

Mitch stood, offering his hand to help her up. Beth took it without hesitation, rising to stand beside him. For a moment, they simply looked at each other in the colored light, savoring the miracle of reconciliation.

"Ready?" he asked.

Beth nodded, her smile steady and sure. "Ready."

Hand in hand, they walked down the aisle toward the sanctuary doors, their steps unhurried. Behind them, the cross hung in silent witness to promises made, to wounds healed, and to love renewed.

And as Mitch pushed open the heavy wooden door, he sent up a silent prayer of gratitude. For Beth's courage. For second chances. For the unwavering certainty that whatever lay ahead, they would face it together—one day, one breath at a time.

EPILOGUE

*O*ne year later...

Beth leaned back into the solid warmth of Mitch's chest, his arm draped comfortably around her shoulders as the porch swing swayed in a gentle rhythm beneath them. Their free hands lay intertwined on her lap, his thumb occasionally tracing the curve of her palm in an absent caress that sent ripples of contentment through her.

Duke snored softly at their feet, his muzzle twitching occasionally in some canine dream. Across from them, Tessa rocked slowly in her chair, bare feet tucked beneath her, while Cody, in a rocking chair beside her, had his arms crossed behind his head.

"All I'm saying," Cody continued, his voice carrying the teasing lilt that had characterized the afternoon's conversation, "is that Earl deserves some kind of medal for putting up with me for a full year without firing me."

"More like Earl deserves our sympathy," Tessa quipped, flicking a peanut shell at her brother. "That poor man had no idea what he was getting into."

Beth laughed, the sound rising easily from her chest. "Actually, I think you two are perfect work companions. I was in there yesterday for picture hooks, and you were explaining the different drill bits to Mrs. Whitaker with such enthusiasm, I thought she might fall asleep standing up. You reminded me of Earl himself."

"Hey!" Cody protested. "That was a very important tutorial. Mrs. Whitaker needs to know the difference between masonry and wood bits."

"She's eighty-three, Cody," Mitch interjected, his chest rumbling with amusement against Beth's back. "I'm pretty sure she was just being polite, listening to you ramble."

"Well, nobody appreciates expertise anymore," Cody grumbled, though his eyes danced with good humor. "Speaking of expertise, Tess, how's that youth pastor of yours? Still 'just friends'?"

Tessa's cheeks flushed pink. "Nathan is fine, thank you very much. And yes, we're just friends."

"Friends who had dinner together three times last week," Mitch pointed out mildly.

"And who I saw holding hands at the Fourth of July picnic," Beth added, grinning as Tessa's blush deepened.

"We were—" Tessa began, then stopped, clearly reconsidering her denial. "Okay, fine. Maybe we're a little more than friends. But we're taking it slow."

"Taking it glacial —more like," Cody teased.

"Not everyone moves at the speed Mitch did," Tessa said. "Some of us prefer to actually get to know someone before diving headfirst into a relationship."

The conversation flowed easily, punctuated by laughter and the creaking of rocking chairs against wooden boards. Beth nestled deeper into Mitch's embrace, her heart swelling with quiet joy. This feeling of belonging and uncomplicated love had become her Sunday afternoon routine over the past year. What had once felt foreign, even intimidating, now wrapped around her like a favorite sweater, familiar and cherished.

The Sunday afternoon gathering at the Baker farmhouse had evolved into a tradition Beth treasured—a few hours of respite between church and the busy week ahead, filled with good food, better company, and the kind of laughter that left your sides aching.

A year ago, she would never have imagined herself here, so completely woven into the fabric of this family. A year ago, her heart had still been armored against the possibility of trust and of genuine connection.

A year ago today, in fact...

"What are you thinking about?" Mitch murmured against her hair, his voice low enough that only she could hear it. "You just got very quiet."

Beth tilted her head to look up at him, taking in the strong line of his jaw, the warmth in his eyes that never failed to make her feel seen, valued, cherished.

"Do you know what today is?" she asked softly.

His brow furrowed slightly, but the grin on his face gave him away. "Hmmm... Sunday, July 15th?"

"It's been exactly one year since I called the sheriff's department to report the shoplifting at Mountain Chic," Beth said, her lips curving into a smile at the memory. "One year since you walked into my boutique, all official and serious."

"I didn't forget. It's been one year since you looked at me like I was crazy for suggesting security cameras."

"I did not!"

"You absolutely did," he insisted, chuckling.

Beth groaned, burying her face against his shoulder. "I was so prickly."

"You were magnificent," Mitch corrected, pressing a kiss to the top of her head. "Strong, independent, and completely determined to handle everything yourself."

"And look how well that turned out," Beth laughed.

Tessa's voice broke into their private moment. "Wait, today is your anniversary?"

"Sort of," Beth replied, straightening slightly but remaining within the circle of Mitch's arm. "Not of dating, but of meeting—or re-meeting, I guess. We'd seen each other around town before, but never really talked until then."

"The infamous boutique theft," Cody nodded sagely. "When Mitch came home that night, he wouldn't shut up about this 'fascinating shop owner'."

"I did not say 'fascinating,'" Mitch protested.

"No, I think the exact word was 'intriguing,'" Cody corrected with a grin. "Which, coming from Mr. Vocabulary-of-a-Rock over here, was practically a sonnet."

Beth felt a pleasant warmth spreading through her chest at the thought of Mitch talking about her that first day. "Really? You never told me that."

Mitch straightened slightly, a new intentness in his gaze as it rested on her face. He gently disentangled himself from her, the swing wobbling slightly with the change in weight distribution. "That day changed everything for me," he said, standing and turning to face her fully.

Beth stared up at him, her heart picking up pace at the serious note in his voice. From the corner of her eye, she noticed Tessa and Cody exchanging a quick glance, but her attention remained fixed on Mitch.

"I remember thinking that the man who had hurt you was the biggest fool on earth," Mitch continued, his expression softening. "And that if I ever got the chance, I'd show you what it means to be truly seen, truly valued and truly loved."

"Mitch…"

Then, in one fluid motion that stole the breath from her lungs, Mitch lowered himself to one knee before her.

Beth's hand flew to her mouth, her eyes widening in shock. Tessa gasped audibly, while Cody leaned forward in his chair, all traces of teasing gone from his face.

"Beth," Mitch said, his voice steady despite the emotion Beth could see swimming in his eyes. He reached into his back jeans pocket and withdrew a small velvet box. "My love."

The world around Beth seemed to blur at the edges, narrowing until there was only Mitch, only this moment, only the thundering of her heart against her ribs.

"A year ago, I knew my life had begun," Mitch said, his voice carrying clearly in the hushed silence that had fallen over the porch. "Every day since then, you've filled my world with more joy, peace, and laughter than I ever thought possible."

He opened the box to reveal a ring that caught the afternoon sunlight in a brilliant flash—a solitaire diamond set in white gold, with tiny, intricate engravings along the band that, upon closer inspection, formed delicate butterfly wings.

"You showed me how to live, how to open my heart fully," Mitch continued, his voice growing thick with emotion. "You are the bravest, kindest, most wonderful woman I know, and you see the best in me, even when I struggle to see it myself."

Tears welled in Beth's eyes, spilling over to trace warm paths down her cheeks. She made no move to wipe them away, too transfixed by the man before her and the words flowing from his heart.

"Remember that butterfly at the waterfall?" Mitch asked, referring to the moment that had changed everything for them. "It was a promise of a new creation. And you, Beth, you are my new beginning, my answered prayer, the most beautiful part of God's plan for me."

A sob caught in Beth's throat, overwhelmed by the memory and the perfect symbolism captured in the ring's design. He'd remembered. Of course he had. Mitch remembered everything that mattered to her.

"I loved you then, I've loved you as we grew closer, and I've loved you through the storms we've weathered together this past year," Mitch said, his voice unwavering despite the moisture gathering in his own eyes. "Now, I want to love you as my wife, for all the days God gives us. I want to build a home together, fill it with love, and wake up next to you every morning."

He took a deep breath, his gaze locked with hers, naked vulnerability and hopeful certainty mingling in their depths. "Beth Rutledge," his voice cracked slightly on her name, "you are my 'always.' Will you marry me?"

For a heartbeat, Beth couldn't speak, couldn't move, could barely breathe through the overwhelming tide of emotion. The past year flashed through her mind in vivid snapshots—their picnic by the creek, their evening at River Bend Vineyard, the painful misunderstanding about Charleston, their reconciliation in the empty sanctuary of Laurel Ridge Community Church. A year of healing, of learning to trust, of falling deeper in love with this extraordinary man who had never wavered, never pushed, never been anything but steadfast and true.

"Oh, Mitch!" she finally managed, her voice breaking on his name. She nodded vigorously, tears streaming freely now. "Yes, of course, I'll marry you! A million times, yes!"

Mitch's face transformed with joy, relief washing over his features as he carefully removed the ring from its velvet nest. With slightly trembling fingers, he slid it onto her left hand, where it nestled perfectly, as though it had always belonged there.

The moment the ring was securely in place, Beth lunged forward, nearly toppling off the swing in her eagerness to reach him. She threw her arms around his neck, burying her face against his shoulder as happy sobs shook her frame. Mitch's arms encircled her waist, lifting her off the swing entirely as he rose to his feet, holding her close against him.

"I love you," she whispered fiercely against his ear. "I love you so very much."

When he finally set her back on her feet, she framed his face between her palms, examining every beloved feature through tear-blurred vision before pulling him down for a kiss that conveyed everything words could not—gratitude, wonder, promise, and above all, a love so deep it seemed to transcend the physical world entirely.

Around them, reality slowly filtered back in—Tessa's sniffling, Cody's enthusiastic "Whoop!" of celebration, Duke's confused barking at the sudden commotion. Beth pulled back slightly. "We are not waiting another year for the wedding, Sheriff Baker!" she declared, laughing through her tears. "The sooner, the better! I've waited long enough to be your wife."

Mitch laughed, his own eyes suspiciously bright. "Whatever you want, my love. As long as it ends with you as Mrs. Baker."

"Mrs. Baker," Beth repeated, testing the sound of it on her tongue. "I like the sound of that."

"Finally!" Cody exclaimed, bounding over to wrap them both in a bear hug that nearly knocked them off their feet. "I was starting to think he'd never work up the nerve. He's been carrying that ring around for weeks!"

"Weeks?" Beth echoed, looking up at Mitch with surprise.

He shrugged, a sheepish smile playing around his lips. "I was waiting for the right moment."

Tessa joined them, her face streaked with happy tears as she embraced Beth tightly. "I'm getting a sister," she whispered, her voice thick with emotion. "The best sister I could have asked for."

"We need to call everyone," Cody announced, already pulling out his phone. "Tessa, call Martha first—you know she'll never forgive us if she's not the first to know."

"And Leslie," Beth added. "She's going to be over the moon."

"What about a fall wedding?" Tessa suggested, wiping at her eyes. "The church looks beautiful in autumn, and we could use harvest colors for the decorations."

"Fall sounds perfect," Beth agreed, unable to stop smiling even as fresh tears threatened.

"Martha will insist on catering," Cody chimed in.

"And she should," Mitch said firmly. "She's family."

The porch filled with excited chatter—wedding dates, guest lists, flower arrangements—the air electric with joy and anticipation. Duke, sensing the excitement, pranced around their feet, tail wagging furiously as he sought attention from each person in turn.

Amidst the happy chaos, Mitch gently drew Beth aside, creating a small pocket of quiet for just the two of them. His fingers intertwined with hers, the new weight of the ring a delicious reminder of what had just transpired.

"Happy?" he asked softly, his eyes searching hers.

Beth placed her free hand against his chest, feeling the steady, strong beat of his heart beneath her palm. The ring caught the light, sending prism-like reflections dancing across his shirt.

"You are my everything," she whispered, the simple words inadequate to express the fullness in her heart, the absolute certainty that this—this man, this love, this future—was God's perfect plan for her life.

Mitch's eyes shone with answering emotion as he bent to press a tender kiss to her forehead. "God is so good," he murmured.

Standing there, surrounded by family, bathed in afternoon sunlight, with the promise of forever gleaming on her finger, Beth knew with unshakable certainty that he was right. God was good, indeed. He had taken her broken pieces and Mitch's steadfast heart and crafted something beautiful—a love story written not in grand gestures or dramatic declarations, but in daily choices, in quiet courage, and in faithful presence.

One year ago, a chance encounter had set them on this path. Now, a lifetime of love stretched before them—a journey they would walk together, hand in hand, one day at a time.

Leave A Review

If you enjoyed this book, please consider leaving an honest review on Amazon

Visit Our Website:

www.tarabaisden.com

Visit Our Amazon Author Page HERE

Find Us On Social Media:

Facebook

Facebook Author Page

Instagram